The Christmas Stories & Poems of George MacDonald

edited by Mark DeBolt

holy fool press
Coldwater, Michigan

for Valerie Kesler

Introductory Note

George MacDonald (1824-1905) was a Scottish minister, who was forced out of his Congregationalist church because of his criticism of Calvinism and especially his universalist doctrine. He then turned to family play-acting and writing for his living. He is best remembered for his children's fantasies, especially *The Princess and the Goblin, The Princess and Curdie, At the Back of the North Wind, The Light Princess* and *Little Daylight*. His adult fantasies *Phantastes* and *Lilith* also continue popular, and his realistic romances have recently seen a revival in edited editions; his *Unspoken Sermons* continue to have an influence on theology. During his lifetime he was good friends with Lewis Carroll, and his oldest son was the first to read the manuscript of *Alice in Wonderland*. His many other literary friends ranged as broadly as Alfred, Lord Tennyson, Mark Twain and Walt Whitman. He was a strong influence on writers such as C. S. Lewis, J. R. R. Tolkien and Madeleine L'Engle. Lewis went so far as to call him his master. His poetry is nearly forgotten, but his *Poetical Works* is available in two volumes from Dodo Press. It is from this that all the poems in this volume are taken except "From Heaven Above" from *Adela Cathcart* and "December 25" from *Diary of an Old Soul*. The stories come from various sources. I believe this volume to be the most complete collection of MacDonald's published Christmas stories and poems available. I hope it entertains, moves and blesses you.

CONTENTS.

Stories

The Shadows

Old Ralph Rinkelmann made his living by comic sketches, and all but lost it again by tragic poems. So he was just the man to be chosen king of the fairies, for in Fairyland the sovereignty is elective.

It is no doubt very strange that fairies should desire to have a mortal king; but the fact is, that with all their knowledge and power, they cannot get rid of the feeling that some men are greater than they are, though they can neither fly nor play tricks. So at such times as there happen to be twice the usual number of sensible electors, such a man as Ralph Rinkelmann gets to be chosen.

They did not mean to insist on his residence; for they needed his presence only on special occasions. But they must get hold of him somehow, first of all, in order to make him king. Once he was crowned, they could get him as often as they pleased; but before this ceremony, there was a difficulty. For it is only between life and death that fairies have power over grown-up mortals, and can carry them off to their country. So they had to wait for an opportunity.

Nor had they to wait long. For old Ralph was taken dreadfully ill; and while hovering between life and death, they carried him off, and crowned him king of Fairyland. But after he was crowned, it was no wonder, considering the state of his health, that he should not be able to sit quite upright on the throne of Fairyland; or that, in consequence, all the gnomes and goblins, and ugly, cruel things that live in the holes and corners of the kingdom, should take advantage of his condition, and run quite wild, playing him, king as he was, all sorts of tricks; crowding about his throne, climbing up the steps, and actually scrambling and quarrelling like mice about his ears and eyes, so that he could see and think of nothing else. But I am not going to tell you anything more about this part of his adventures just at present. By strong and sustained efforts, he succeeded, after much trouble and suffering, in reducing his rebellious subjects to order. They all vanished to their respective holes and corners; and King Ralph, coming to himself, found himself in his bed, half propped up with pillows.

But the room was full of dark creatures, which gambolled about in the firelight in such a strange, huge, though noiseless fashion, that he thought at first that some of his rebellious goblins had not been subdued with the rest, but had followed him beyond the bounds of Fairyland into his own private house in London. How else could these mad, grotesque hippopotamus-calves make their ugly appearance in Ralph Rinkelmann's bedroom? But he soon found out that although they were like the underground goblins, they were very different as well, and would require quite different treatment. He felt convinced that they were his subjects too, but that he must have overlooked them somehow at his coronation—if indeed they had been present; for he could not recollect that he had seen anything just like them before. He resolved, therefore, to pay particular attention to their habits, ways, and characters; else he saw plainly that they would soon be too much for him; as indeed this intrusion into his chamber, where Mrs. Rinkelmann, who must be queen if he was king, sat taking some tea by the fireside, evidently foreshadowed. But she, perceiving that he was looking about him with a more composed expression than his face had worn for many days, started up, and came quickly and quietly to his side, and her face was bright with gladness. Whereupon the fire burned up more cheerily; and the figures became more composed and respectful in their behaviour, retreating towards the wall like well-trained attendants. Then the king of Fairyland had some tea and dry toast, and leaning back on his pillows, nearly fell asleep; but not quite, for he still watched the intruders.

Presently the queen left the room to give some of the young princes and princesses their tea; and the fire burned lower, and behold, the figures grew as black and as mad in their gambols as ever! Their favourite games seemed to be *Hide and Seek; Touch and Go; Grin and Vanish:* and many other such; and all in the king's bedchamber, too; so that it was quite alarming. It was almost as bad as if the house had been haunted by certain creatures which shall be nameless in a fairy story, because with them Fairyland will not willingly have much to do.

"But it is a mercy that they have their slippers on!" said the king to himself; for his head ached.

As he lay back, with his eyes half shut and half open, too tired to pay attention to their games, but, on the whole, considerably more amused than offended with the liberties they took, for they seemed good-natured creatures, and more frolicsome than positively ill-mannered, he became suddenly aware that two of them had stepped forward from the walls, upon which, after the manner of great spiders, most of them preferred sprawling, and now stood in the middle of the floor at the foot of his majesty's bed, becking and bowing and ducking in the most grotesque obsequious manner; while every now and then they turned solemnly round upon one heel, evidently considering that motion the highest token of homage they could show.

"What do you want?" said the king.

"That it may please your majesty to be better acquainted with us," answered they. "We are your majesty's subjects."

"I know you are. I shall be most happy," answered the king.

"We are not what your majesty takes us for, though. We are not so foolish as your majesty thinks us."

"It is impossible to take you for anything that I know of," rejoined the king, who wished to make them talk, and said whatever came uppermost;—"for soldiers, sailors, or anything: you will not stand still long enough. I suppose you really belong to the fire brigade; at least, you keep putting its light out."

"Don't jest, please your majesty." And as they said the words—for they both spoke at once throughout the interview—they performed a grave somerset towards the king.

"Not jest!" retorted he; "and with you? Why, you do nothing but jest. What are you?"

"The Shadows, sire. And when we do jest, sire, we always jest in earnest. But perhaps your majesty does not see us distinctly."

"I see you perfectly well," returned the king.

"Permit me, however," rejoined one of the Shadows; and as he spoke he approached the king; and lifting a dark forefinger, he drew it lightly but carefully across the ridge of his forehead, from temple to temple. The king felt the soft gliding touch go, like water, into every hollow, and over the top of every height of that mountain-chain of thought. He had involuntarily closed his eyes during the operation, and when he unclosed them again, as soon as the finger was withdrawn, he found they were opened in more senses than one. The room appeared to have extended itself on all sides, till he could not exactly see where the walls were; and all about it stood the Shadows motionless. They were tall and solemn; rather awful, indeed, in their appearance, notwithstanding many remarkable traits of grotesqueness, for they looked just like the pictures of puritans drawn by Cavaliers, with long arms, and very long, thin legs, from which hung large loose feet, while in their countenances length of chin and nose predominated. The solemnity of their mien, however, overcame all the oddity of their form, so that they were very *eerie* indeed to look at, dressed as they were in funereal black. But a single glance was all that the king was allowed to have; for the former operator waved his dusky palm across his vision, and once more the king saw only the fire-lighted walls, and dark shapes flickering about upon them. The two who had spoken for the rest seemed likewise to have vanished. But at last the king discovered them, standing one on each side of the fireplace. They kept close to the chimney-wall, and talked to each other across the length of the chimney-piece, thus avoiding the direct rays of the fire, which, though necessary to their appearing to human eyes, do not agree with them at all—much less give birth to them, as the king was soon to learn. After a few minutes they again approached the bed, and spoke thus:—

"It is now getting dark, please your majesty. We mean, out of doors in the snow. Your majesty may see, from where he is lying, the cold light of its great winding-sheet—a famous carpet for the Shadows to dance upon, your majesty. All our brothers and sisters will be at church now, before going to their night's work."

"Do they always go to church before they go to work?"

"They always go to church first."

"Where is the church?"

"In Iceland. Would your majesty like to see it?"

"How can I go and see it, when, as you know very well, I am ill in bed? Besides, I should be sure to take cold in a frosty night like this, even if I put on the blankets, and took the feather-bed for a muff."

A sort of quivering passed over their faces, which seemed their mode of laughing. The whole shape of the face shook and fluctuated as if it had been some dark fluid; till, by slow degrees of gathering calm, it settled into its former rest. Then one of them drew aside the curtains of the bed, and the window-curtains not having been yet drawn, the king beheld the white glimmering night outside, struggling with the heaps of darkness, that tried to quench it; and the heavens full of stars, flashing and sparkling like live jewels. The other Shadow went towards the fire and vanished in it.

Scores of Shadows immediately began an insane dance all about the room; disappearing, one after the other, through the uncovered window, and gliding darkly away over the face of the white snow; for the window looked at once on a field of snow. In a few moments the room was quite cleared of them; but instead of being relieved by their absence, the king felt immediately as if he were in a dead-house, and could hardly breathe for the sense of emptiness and desolation that fell upon him. But as he lay looking out on the snow, which stretched blank and wide before him, he spied in the distance a long dark line which drew nearer and nearer, and showed itself at last to be all the Shadows, walking in a double row, and carrying in the midst of them something like a bier.

They vanished under the window, but soon reappeared, having somehow climbed up the wall of the house; for they entered in perfect order by the window, as if melting through the transparency of the glass.

They still carried the bier or litter. It was covered with richest furs, and skins of gorgeous wild beasts, whose eyes were replaced with sapphires and emeralds, that glittered and gleamed in the fire and snow light. The outermost skin sparkled with frost, but the inside ones were soft and warm and dry as the down under a swan's wing. The Shadows approached the bed, and set the litter upon it. Then a number of them brought a huge fur robe, and wrapping it round the king, laid him on the litter in the midst of the furs. Nothing could be more gentle and respectful than the way in which they moved him; and he never thought of refusing to go. Then they put something on his head, and, lifting the litter, carried him once round the room, to fall into order. As he passed the mirror he saw that he was covered with royal ermine, and that his head wore a wonderful crown of gold, set with none but red stones: rubies and carbuncles and garnets, and others whose names he could not tell, glowed gloriously around his head, like the salamanderine essence of all the Christmas fires over the world. A sceptre lay beside him—a rod of ebony, surmounted by a cone-shaped diamond, which, cut in a hundred facets, flashed all the hues of the rainbow, and threw coloured gleams on every side, that looked like Shadows too, but more ethereal than those that bore him. Then the Shadows rose gently to the window, passed through it, and sinking slowly upon the field of outstretched snow, commenced an orderly gliding rather than march along the frozen surface. They took it by turns to bear the king, as they sped with the swiftness of thought, in a straight line towards the north. The pole-star rose above their heads with visible rapidity; for indeed they moved quite as fast as sad thoughts, though not with all the speed of happy desires. England and Scotland slid past the litter of the king of the Shadows. Over rivers and lakes they skimmed and glided. They climbed the high mountains, and crossed the valleys with a fearless bound; till they came to John-o'-Groat's house and the Northern Sea. The sea was not frozen; for all the stars shone out as clear of the deeps below as they shone out of the deeps above; and the bearers slid along the blue-gray surface, with never a furrow in their track, so pure was the water beneath, that the king saw neither surface, bottom, nor substance to it, and seemed to be gliding only through the blue sphere of heaven, with the stars above him, and the stars below him, and between the stars and him nothing but an emptiness, where, for the first time in his life, his soul felt that it had room enough.

At length they reached the rocky shores of Iceland. There they landed, still pursuing their journey. All this time the king felt no cold; for the red stones in his crown kept him warm, and the emerald and sapphire eyes of the wild beasts kept the frosts from settling upon his litter.

Oftentimes upon their way they had to pass through forests, caverns, and rock-shadowed paths, where it was so dark that at first the king feared he should lose his Shadows altogether. But as soon as they entered such places, the diamond in his sceptre began to shine, and glow, and flash, sending out streams of light of all the colours that painter's soul could dream of; in which light the Shadows grew livelier and stronger than ever, speeding through the dark ways with an all but blinding swiftness. In the light of the diamond, too, some of their forms became more simple and human, while others seemed only to break out into a yet more untamable absurdity. Once, as they passed through a cave, the king actually saw some of their eyes—strange shadow-eyes: he had never seen any of their eyes before. But at the same moment when he saw their eyes, he knew their faces too, for they turned them full upon him for an instant; and the other Shadows, catching sight of these, shrank and shivered, and nearly vanished. Lovely faces they were; but the king was very thoughtful after he saw them, and continued rather troubled all the rest of the journey. He could not account for those faces being there, and the faces of the Shadows, too, with living eyes.

But he soon found that amongst the Shadows a man must learn never to be surprised at anything; for if he does not, he will soon grow quite stupid, in consequence of the endless recurrence of surprises.

At last they climbed up the bed of a little stream, and then, passing through a narrow rocky defile, came out suddenly upon the side of a mountain, overlooking a blue frozen lake in the very heart of mighty hills. Overhead, the *aurora borealis* was shivering and flashing like a battle of ten thousand spears. Underneath, its beams passed faintly over the blue ice and the sides of the snow-clad mountains, whose tops shot up like huge icicles all about, with here and there a star sparkling on the very tip of one. But as the northern lights in the sky above, so wavered and quivered, and shot hither and thither, the Shadows on the surface of the lake below; now gathering in groups, and now shivering asunder; now covering the whole surface of the lake, and anon condensed into one dark knot in the centre. Every here and there on the white mountains might be seen two or three shooting away towards the tops, to vanish beyond them, so that the number was gradually, though not visibly, diminishing.

"Please your majesty," said the Shadows, "this is our church—the Church of the Shadows."

And so saying, the king's body-guard set down the litter upon a rock, and plunged into the multitudes below. They soon returned, however, and bore the king down into the middle of the lake. All the Shadows came crowding round him, respectfully but fearlessly; and sure never was such a grotesque assembly revealed itself before to mortal eyes. The king had seen all kinds of gnomes, goblins, and kobolds at his coronation; but they were quite rectilinear figures compared with the insane lawlessness of form in which the Shadows rejoiced; and the wildest gambols of the former were orderly dances of ceremony beside the apparently aimless and wilful contortions of figure, and metamorphoses of shape, in which the latter indulged. They retained, however, all the time, to the surprise of the king, an identity, each of his own type, inexplicably perceptible through every change. Indeed, this preservation of the primary idea of each form was more wonderful than the bewildering and ridiculous alterations to which the form itself was every moment subjected.

"What are you?" said the king, leaning on his elbow, and looking around him.

"The Shadows, your majesty," answered several voices at once.

"What Shadows?"

"The human Shadows. The Shadows of men, and women, and their children."

"Are you not the shadows of chairs and tables, and pokers and tongs, just as well?"

At this question a strange jarring commotion went through the assembly with a shock. Several of the figures shot up as high as the aurora, but instantly settled down again to human size, as if overmastering their feelings, out of respect to him who had roused them. One who had bounded to the highest visible icy peak, and as suddenly returned, now elbowed his way through the rest, and made himself spokesman for them during the remaining of the dialogue.

"Excuse our agitation, your majesty," said he. "I see your majesty has not yet thought proper to make himself acquainted with our nature and habits."

"I wish to do so now," replied the king.

"We are the Shadows," repeated the Shadow solemnly.

"Well?" said the king.

"We do not often appear to men."

"Ha!" said the king.

"We do not belong to the sunshine at all. We go through it unseen, and only by a passing chill do men recognize an unknown presence."

"Ha!" said the king again.

"It is only in the twilight of the fire, or when one man or woman is alone with a single candle, or when any number of people are all feeling the same thing at once, making them one, that we show ourselves, and the truth of things."

"Can that be true that loves the night?" said the king.

"The darkness is the nurse of light," answered the Shadow.

"Can that be true which mocks at forms?" said the king.

"Truth rides abroad in shapeless storms," answered the Shadow.

"Ha! ha!" thought Ralph Rinkelmann, "it rhymes. The Shadow caps my questions with his answers. Very strange!" And he grew thoughtful again.

The Shadow was the first to resume.

"Please your majesty, may we present our petition?"

"By all means," replied the king. "I am not well enough to receive it in proper state."

"Never mind, your majesty. We do not care for much ceremony; and indeed none of us are quite well at present. The subject of our petition weighs upon us."

"Go on," said the king.

"Sire," began the Shadow, "our very existence is in danger. The various sorts of artificial light, both in houses and in men, women, and children, threaten to end our being. The use and the disposition of gas-lights, especially high in the centres, blind the eyes by which alone we can be perceived. We are all but banished from towns. We are driven into villages and lonely houses, chiefly old farm-houses, out of which, even, our friends the fairies are fast disappearing. We therefore petition our king, by the power of his art, to restore us to our rights in the house itself, and in the hearts of its inhabitants."

"But," said the king, "you frighten the children."

"Very seldom, your majesty; and then only for their good. We seldom seek to frighten anybody. We mostly want to make people silent and thoughtful; to awe them a little, your majesty."

"You are much more likely to make them laugh," said the king.

"Are we?" said the Shadow.

And approaching the king one step, he stood quite still for a moment. The diamond of the king's sceptre shot out a vivid flame of violet light, and the king stared at the Shadow in silence, and his lip quivered. He never told what he saw then; but he would say:

"Just fancy what it might be if *some* flitting thoughts were to persist in staying to be looked at."

"It is only," resumed the Shadow, "when our thoughts are not fixed upon any particular object, that our bodies are subject to all the vagaries of elemental influences. Gradually, amongst worldly men and frivolous women, we only attach ourselves to some article of furniture or of dress; and they never doubt that we are mere foolish and vague results of the dashing of the waves of the light against the solid forms of which their houses are full. We do not care to tell them the truth, for they would never see it. But the worldly man—or the frivolous woman—and then—"

At each of the pauses indicated, the mass of Shadows throbbed and heaved with emotion; but they soon settled again into comparative stillness. Once more the Shadow addressed himself to speak. But suddenly they all looked up, and the king, following their gaze, saw that the aurora had begun to pale.

"The moon is rising," said the Shadow. "As soon as she looks over the mountains into the valley, we must be gone, for we have plenty to do by the moon: we are powerful in her light. But if your majesty will come here to-morrow night, your majesty may learn a great deal more about us, and judge for himself whether it be fit to accord our petition; for then will be our grand annual assembly, in which we report to our chiefs the things we have attempted, and the good or bad success we have had."

"If you send for me," returned the king, "I will come."

Ere the Shadow could reply, the tip of the moon's crescent horn peeped up from behind an icy pinnacle, and one slender ray fell on the lake. It shone upon no Shadows. Ere the eye of the king could again seek the earth after beholding the first brightness of the moon's resurrection, they had vanished; and the surface of the lake glittered cold and blue in the pale moonlight.

There the king lay, alone in the midst of the frozen lake, with the moon staring at him. But at length he heard from somewhere a voice that he knew.

"Will you take another cup of tea, dear?" said Mrs. Rinkelmann.

And Ralph, coming slowly to himself, found that he was lying in his own bed.

"Yes, I will," he answered; "and rather a large piece of toast, if you please; for I have been a long journey since I saw you last."

"He has not come to himself quite," said Mrs. Rinkelmann, between her and herself.

"You would be rather surprised," continued Ralph, "if I told you where I have been."

"I dare say I should," responded his wife.

"Then I will tell you," rejoined Ralph.

But at that moment a great Shadow bounced out of the fire with a single huge leap, and covered the whole room. Then it settled in one corner, and Ralph saw it shaking its fist at him from the end of a preposterous arm. So he took the hint, and held his peace. And it was as well for him. For I happen to know something about the Shadows too; and I know that if he had told his wife all about it just then, they would not have sent for him the following evening.

But as the king, after finishing his tea and toast, lay and looked about him, the Shadows dancing in his room seemed to him odder and more inexplicable than ever. The whole chamber was full of mystery. So it generally was, but now it was more mysterious than ever. After all that he had seen in the Shadow-church, his own room and its shadows were yet more wonderful and unintelligible than those.

This made it the more likely that he had seen a true vision; for instead of making common things look commonplace, as a false vision would have done, it had made common things disclose the wonderful that was in them.

"The same applies to all art as well," thought Ralph Rinkelmann.

The next afternoon, as the twilight was growing dusky, the king lay wondering whether or not the Shadows would fetch him again. He wanted very much to go, for he had enjoyed the journey exceedingly, and he longed, besides, to hear some of the Shadows tell their stories. But the darkness grew deeper and deeper, and the Shadows did not come. The cause was, that Mrs. Rinkelmann sat by the fire in the gloaming; and they could not carry off the king while she was there. Some of them tried to frighten her away by playing the oddest pranks on the walls, the floor, and ceiling; but altogether without effect: the queen only smiled, for she had a good conscience. Suddenly, however, a dreadful scream was heard from the nursery, and Mrs. Rinkelmann rushed up-stairs to see what was the matter. No sooner had she gone than the two warders of the chimney-corner stepped out into the middle of the room, and said, in a low voice,—

"Is your majesty ready?"

"Have you no hearts?" said the king; "or are they as black as your faces? Did you not hear the child scream? I must know what is the matter with her before I go."

"Your majesty may keep his mind easy on that point," replied the warders. "We had tried everything we could think of to get rid of her majesty the queen, but without effect. So a young madcap Shadow, half against the will of the older ones of us, slipped upstairs into the nursery; and has, no doubt, succeeded in appalling the baby, for he is very lithe and long-legged.—Now, your majesty."

"I will have no such tricks played in my nursery," said the king, rather angrily. "You might put the child beside itself."

"Then there would be twins, your majesty. And we rather like twins."

"None of your miserable jesting! You might put the child out of her wits."

"Impossible, sire; for she has not got into them yet."

"Go away," said the king.

"Forgive us, your majesty. Really, it will do the child good; for that Shadow will, all her life, be to her a symbol of what is ugly and bad. When she feels in danger of hating or envying any one, that Shadow will come back to her mind and make her shudder."

"Very well," said the king. "I like that. Let us go."

The Shadows went through the same ceremonies and preparations as before; during which, the young Shadow before-mentioned contrived to make such grimaces as kept the baby in terror, and the queen in the nursery, till all was ready. Then with a bound that doubled him up against the ceiling, and a kick of his legs six feet out behind him, he vanished through the nursery door, and reached the king's bed-chamber just in time to take his place with the last who were melting through the window in the rear of the litter, and settling down upon the snow beneath. Away they went as before, a gliding blackness over the white carpet. And it was Christmas-eve.

When they came in sight of the mountain-lake, the king saw that it was crowded over its whole surface with a changeful intermingling of Shadows. They were all talking and listening alternately, in pairs, trios, and groups of every size. Here and there, large companies were absorbed in attention to one elevated above the rest, not in a pulpit, or on a platform, but on the stilts of his own legs, elongated for the nonce.

The aurora, right overhead, lighted up the lake and the sides of the mountains, by sending down from the zenith, nearly to the surface of the lake, great folded vapours, luminous with all the colours of a faint rainbow.

Many, however, as the words were that passed on all sides, not a shadow of a sound reached the ears of the king: the shadow-speech could not enter his corporeal organs. One of his guides, however, seeing that the king wanted to hear and could not, went through a strange manipulation of his head and ears; after which he could hear perfectly, though still only the voice to which, for the time, he directed his attention. This, however, was a great advantage, and one which the king longed to carry back with him to the world of men.

The king now discovered that this was not merely the church of the Shadows, but their news-exchange at the same time. For, as the Shadows have no writing or printing, the only way in which they can make each other acquainted with their doings and thinkings, is to meet and talk at this word-mart and parliament of shades. And as, in the world, people read their favourite authors, and listen to their favourite speakers, so here the Shadows seek their favourite Shadows, listen to their adventures, and hear generally what they have to say.

Feeling quite strong, the king rose and walked about amongst them, wrapped in his ermine robe, with his red crown on his head, and his diamond sceptre in his hand. Every group of Shadows to which he drew near, ceased talking as soon as they saw him approach: but at a nod they went on again directly, conversing and relating and commenting, as if no one was there of other kind or higher rank than themselves. So the king heard a good many stories. At some of them he laughed, and at some of them he cried. But if the stories that the Shadows told were printed, they would make a book that no publisher could produce fast enough to satisfy the buyers. I will record some of the things that the king heard, for he told them to me soon after. In fact, I was for some time his private secretary.

"I made him confess before a week was over," said a gloomy old Shadow.

"But what was the good of that?" rejoined a pert one. "That could not undo what was done."

"Yes, it could."

"What! bring the dead to life?"

"No; but comfort the murderer. I could not bear to see the pitiable misery he was in. He was far happier with the rope round his neck, than he was with the purse in his pocket. I saved him from killing himself too."

"How did you make him confess?"

"Only by wallowing on the wall a little."

"How could that make him tell?"

"He knows."

The Shadow was silent; and the king turned to another, who was preparing to speak.

"I made a fashionable mother repent."

"How?" broke from several voices, in whose sound was mingled a touch of incredulity.

"Only by making a little coffin on the wall," was the reply.

"Did the fashionable mother confess too?"

"She had nothing more to confess than everybody knew."

"What did everybody know then?"

"That she might have been kissing a living child, when she followed a dead one to the grave.—The next will fare better."

"I put a stop to a wedding," said another.

"Horrid shade!" remarked a poetic imp

"How?" said others. "Tell us how."

"Only by throwing a darkness, as if from the branch of a sconce, over the forehead of a fair girl.—They are not married yet, and I do not think they will be. But I loved the youth who loved her. How he started! It was a revelation to him."

"But did it not deceive him?"

"Quite the contrary."

"But it was only a shadow from the outside, not a shadow coming from the soul of the girl."

"Yes, you may say so. But it was all that was wanted to make the meaning of her forehead manifest—yes, of her whole face, which had now and then, in the pauses of his passion, perplexed the youth. All of it, curled nostrils, pouting lips, projecting chin, instantly fell into harmony with the darkness between her eyebrows. The youth understood it in a moment, and went home miserable. And they're not married *yet."*

"I caught a toper alone, over his magnum of port," said a very dark Shadow; "and didn't give it him! I made *delirium tremens* first; and then I settled into a funeral, passing slowly along the length of the opposite wall. I gave him plenty of plumes and mourning coaches. And then I gave him a funeral service, but I could not manage to make the surplice white, which was all the better for such a sinner. The wretch stared till his face passed from purple to grey, and actually left his fifth glass only, unfinished, and took refuge with his wife and children in the drawing-room, much to their surprise. I believe he actually drank a cup of tea; and although I have often looked in since, I have never caught him again, drinking alone at least."

"But does he drink less? Have you done him any good?"

"I hope so; but I am sorry to say I can't feel sure about it."

"Humph! Humph! Humph!" grunted various shadow throats.

"I had such fun once!" cried another. "I made such game of a young clergyman!"

"You have no right to make game of any one."

"Oh yes, I have—when it was for his good. He used to study his sermons—where do you think?"

"In his study, of course. Where else should it be?"

"Yes and no. Guess again."

"Out amongst the faces in the streets?"

"Guess again."

"In still green places in the country?"

"Guess again."

"In old books?"

"No, no. Tell us."

"In the looking-glass. Ha! ha! ha!"

"He was fair game; fair shadow game."

"I thought so. And I made such fun of him one night on the wall! He had sense enough to see that it was himself, and very like an ape. So he got ashamed, turned the mirror with its face to the wall, and thought a little more about his people, and a little less about himself. I was very glad; for, please your majesty,"—and here the speaker turned towards the king—"we don't like the creatures that live in the mirrors. You call them ghosts, don't you?"

Before the king could reply, another had commenced. But the story about the clergyman had made the king wish to hear one of the shadow-sermons. So he turned towards a long Shadow, who was preaching to a very quiet and listening crowd. He was just concluding his sermon.

"Therefore, dear Shadows, it is the more needful that we love one another as much as we can, because that is not much. We have no such excuse for not loving mortals have, for we do not die like them. I suppose it is the thought of that death that makes them hate so much. Then again, we go to sleep all day, most of us, and not in the night, as men do. And you know that we forget everything that happened the night before; therefore, we ought to love well, for the love is short. Ah! dear Shadow, whom I love now with all my shadowy soul, I shall not love thee to-morrow eve, I shall not know thee; I shall pass thee in the crowd and never dream that the Shadow whom I now love is near me then. Happy Shades! for we only remember our tales until we have told them here, and then they vanish in the shadow-churchyard, where we bury only our dead selves. Ah! brethren, who would be a man and remember? Who would be a man and weep? We ought indeed to love one another, for we alone inherit oblivion; we alone are renewed with eternal birth; we alone have no gathered weight of years. I will tell you the awful fate of one Shadow who rebelled against his nature, and sought to remember the past. He said, 'I *will* remember this eve.' He fought with the genial influences of kindly sleep when the sun rose on the awful dead day of light; and although he could not keep quite awake, he dreamed of the foregone eve, and he never forgot his dream. Then he tried again the next night, and the next, and the next; and he tempted another Shadow to try it with him. But at last their awful fate overtook them; for, instead of continuing to be Shadows, they began to cast shadows, as foolish men say; and so they thickened and thickened till they vanished out of our world. They are now condemned to walk the earth a man and a woman, with death behind them, and memories within them. Ah, brother Shades! let us love one another, for we shall soon forget. We are not men, but Shadows."

The king turned away, and pitied the poor Shadows far more than they pitied men.

"Oh! how we played with a musician one night," exclaimed a Shadow in another group, to which the king had first directed a passing thought.—"Up and down we went, like the hammers and dampers of his piano. But he took his revenge on us. For after he had watched us for half an hour in the twilight, he wrote and went to the instrument and played a shadow-dance that fixed us all in sound for ever. Each could tell the very notes meant for him; and as long as he played we could not stop, but went on dancing and dancing after the music, just as the magician—I mean the musician—pleased. And he punished us well; for he nearly danced us off our legs and out of shape into tired heaps of collapsed and palpating darkness. We won't go near him for some time again, if we can only remember it. He had been very miserable all day, he was so poor; and we could not think of any way of comforting him except making him laugh. We did not succeed, with our wildest efforts, after all; for his shadow-dance got him into notice, and he is quite popular now, and making money fast.—If he does not take care, we shall have other work to do with him by-and-by, poor fellow!"

"I and some others did the same for a poor play-writer once. He had a Christmas piece to write, and being an original genius, it was not so easy for him to find a subject as it is for most of his class. I saw the trouble he was in, and collecting a few stray Shadows, we acted, in dumb show of course, the funniest bit of nonsense we could think of; and it was quite successful. The poor fellow watched every motion, roaring with laughter at us, and delight at the ideas we put into his head. He turned it all into words, and scenes, and actions; and the piece came off with a splendid success."

"But how long we have to look for a chance of doing anything worth doing!" said a long, thin, especially lugubrious Shadow. "I have only done one thing worth telling about since we met last. But I am proud of that."

"What was it? What was it?" rose from twenty voices.

"I crept into a dining room, one twilight, soon after Christmas day. I had been drawn thither by the glow of a bright fire shining through red window-curtains. At first I thought there was no one there, and was on the point of leaving the room and going out again into the snowy street, when I suddenly caught the sparkle of eyes. I found that they belonged to a little boy who lay very still on a sofa. I crept into a dark corner by the sideboard, and watched him. He seemed very sad, and did nothing but stare into the fire. At last he sighed out,—'I wish mamma would come home.' 'Poor boy!' thought I, 'there is no help for that but mamma.' Yet I would try to while away the time for him. So out of my corner I stretched a long shadow-arm, reaching all across the ceiling, and pretended to make a grab at him. He was rather frightened at first; but he was a brave boy, and soon saw that it was all a joke. So when I did it again, he made a clutch at me, and then we had such fun! For though he often sighed and wished mamma would come home, he always began again with me; and on we went with the wildest game. At last his mother's knock came to the door, and, starting up in delight, he rushed into the hall to meet her, and forgot all about poor black me. But I did not mind that in the least; for when I glided out after him into the hall, I was well repaid for my trouble by hearing his mother say to him,—'What Shadow can that be gliding so quickly?' And Charlie answered with a merry laugh,—'Oh! mamma, I suppose it must be the funny shadow that has been playing such games with me all the time you were out.' As soon as the door was shut, I crept along the wall and looked in at the dining-room window. And I heard his mamma say, as she led him into the room,—'What an imagination the boy has!' Ha! ha! ha! Then she looked at him, and the tears came in her eyes; and she stooped down over him, and I heard the sounds of a mingling kiss and sob."

"I always look for nurseries full of children," said another; "and this winter I have been very fortunate. I am sure children belong especially to us. One evening, looking about in a great city, I saw through the window into a large nursery, where the odious gas had not yet been lighted. Round the fire sat a company of the most delightful children I had ever seen. They were waiting patiently for their tea. It was too good an opportunity to be lost. I hurried away, and gathering together twenty of the best Shadows I could find, returned in a few moments; and entering the nursery, we danced on the walls one of our best dances. To be sure it was mostly extemporized; but I managed to keep it in harmony by singing this song, which I made as we went on. Of course the children could not hear it; they only saw the motions that answered to it; but with them they seemed to be very much delighted indeed, as I shall presently prove to you. This was the song:—

> *Swing, swang, swingle, swuff!*
> *Flicker, flacker, fling, fluff!*
> > *Thus we go,*
> > *To and fro;*
> > *Here and there,*
> > *Everywhere,*
> > *Born and bred;*
> > *Never dead,*
> > > *Only gone.*
>
> *'On! Come on.*
> *Looming, glooming,*
> *Spreading, fuming,*
> *Shattering, scattering,*
> *All our life*
> *Is a strife,*
> *And a wearying one for rest*
> *On the darkness' friendly breast.*

'Joining, splitting,
  Rising, sitting,
  Laughing, shaking,
  Sides all aching,
Grumble, grim, and gruff.
Swingle, swangle, swuff!

   'Now a knot of darkness;
    Now dissolved gloom;
  Now a pall of blackness
    Hiding all the room.
Flicker, flacker, fluff!
Black, and black enough!

   'Dancing now like demons;
    Lying like the dead;
  Gladly would we stop it,
    And go back to bed!
But our work we still must do,
Shadow men, as well as you.

   'Rooting, rising, shooting,
    Heaving, sinking, creeping;
  Hid in corners crooning;
    Splitting, poling, leaping,
  Gathering, towering, swooning.
    When we're lurking,
    Yet we're working,
For our labor we must do,
Shadow men, as well as you.
    Flicker, flacker, fling, fluff!
  Swing, swang, swingle, swuff!'

"'How thick the Shadows are!' said one of the children—a thoughtful little girl.

"'I wonder where they come from,' said a dreamy little boy.

"'I think they grow out of the wall,' answered the little girl; 'for I have been watching them come; first one, and then another, and then a whole lot of them. I am sure they grow out of the walls.'

"'Perhaps they have papas and mammas,' said an older boy, with a smile.

"'Yes, yes, and the doctor brings them in his pocket,' said another, a consequential little maiden.

"'No, I'll tell you,' said the older boy: they're ghosts.'

"'But ghosts are white.'

"'Oh! but these have got black coming down the chimney.'

"'No,' said a curious-looking, white-faced boy of fourteen, who had been reading by the firelight, and had stopped to hear the little ones talk; 'they're body ghosts; they're not soul ghosts.'

"A silence followed, broken by the first, the dreamy-eyed boy, who said,—

"'I hope they didn't make me'; at which they all burst out laughing.

"Just then the nurse brought in their tea, and when she proceeded to light the gas we vanished."

"I stopped a murder," cried another.

"How? How? How?"

"I will tell you. I had been lurking about a sick room for some time, where a miser lay, apparently dying. I did not like the place at all, but felt as if I should be wanted there. There were plenty of lurking-places about, for the room was full of all sorts of furniture, especially cabinets, chests, and presses. I believe he had in that room every bit of the property he had spent a long life in gathering. I found that he had gold and gold in those places; for one night, when his nurse was away, he crept out of bed, mumbling and shaking, and managed to open one of the chests, though he nearly fell down with the effort. I was peeping over his shoulder, and such a gleam of gold fell upon me, that it nearly killed me. But hearing his nurse coming, he slammed the lid down, and I recovered.

"I tried very hard, but I could not do him any good. For although I made all sorts of shapes on the walls and ceiling, representing evil deeds that he had done, of which there were plenty to choose from, I could make no shapes on his brain or conscience. He had no eyes for anything but gold. And it so happened that his nurse had neither eyes nor heart for anything else either.

"One day, as she was seated beside his bed, but where he could not see her, stirring some gruel in a basin, to cool it for him, I saw her take a little phial from her bosom, and I knew by the expression of her face both what it was and what she was going to do with it. Fortunately the cork was a little hard to get out, and this gave me one moment to think.

"The Room was so crowded with all sorts of things, that although there were no curtains on the four-post bed to hide from the miser the sight of his precious treasures, there was yet one small part of the ceiling suitable for casting myself upon in the shape I wished to assume. And this spot was hard to reach. But having discovered that upon this very place lay a dull gleam of firelight thrown from a strange old dusty mirror that stood away in the corner, I got in front of the fire, spied where the mirror was, threw myself upon it, and bounded from its face upon the oval pool of dim light on the ceiling, assuming, as I passed, the shape of an old stooping hag, who poured something from a phial into a basin. I made the handle of the spoon with my own nose, ha! ha!"

And the shadow-hand caressed the shadow-tip of the shadow-nose, before the shadow-tongue resumed.

"The old miser saw me: he would not taste the gruel that night, although his nurse coaxed and scolded till they were both weary. She pretended to taste it herself, and to think it very good; but at last retired into a corner, and after making as she was eating it, took care to pour it all in the ashes."

"But she must either succeed, or starve him, at last," interposed a Shadow.

"I will tell you."

"And," interposed another, "he was not worth saving."

"He might repent," suggested a third, who was more benevolent.

"No chance of that," returned the former. "Misers never do. The love of money has less in it to cure itself than any other wickedness into which wretched men can fall. What a mercy it is to be born a Shadow! Wickedness does not stick to us. What do we care for gold!—Rubbish!"

"Amen! Amen! Amen!" came from a hundred shadow-voices.

"You should have let her murder him, and so you would have been quit of him."

"And besides, how was he to escape at last? He could never get rid of her, you know."

"I was going to tell you," resumed the narrator, "only you had so many shadow-remarks to make, that you would not let me."

"Go on; go on."

"There was a little grandchild who used to come and see him sometimes—the only creature the miser cared for. Her mother was his daughter; but the old man would never see her, because she had married against his will. Her husband was now dead, but he had not forgiven her yet. After the shadow he had seen, however, he said to himself, as he lay awake that night—I saw the words on his face—'How shall I get rid of that old devil? If I don't eat, I shall die; and if I do eat I shall be poisoned. I wish little Mary would come. Ah! her mother would never have served me so.' He lay awake, thinking such things over and over again, all night long, and I stood watching him from a dark corner, till the dayspring came and shook me out. When I came back next night, the room was tidy and clean. His own daughter, a sad-faced but beautiful woman, sat by his bedside; and little Mary was curled up on the floor by the fire, imitating us, by making queer shadows on the ceiling with her twisted hands. But she could not think however they got there. And no wonder, for I helped her to some very unaccountable ones."

"I have a story about a granddaughter, too," said another, the moment that speaker ceased.

"Tell it. Tell it."

"Last Christmas-day," he began, "I and a troop of us set out in the twilight to find some house where we could all have something to do; for we had made up our minds to act together. We tried several, but found objections to them all. At last we espied a large lonely country-house, and hastening to it, we found great preparations making for the Christmas dinner. We rushed into it, scampered all over it, and made up our minds in a moment that it would do. We amused ourselves in the nursery first, where there were several children being dressed for dinner. We generally do go to the nursery first, your majesty. This time we were especially charmed with a little girl about five years old, who clapped her hands and danced about with delight at the antics we performed; and we said we would do something for her if we had a chance. The company began to arrive; and at every arrival, we rushed to the hall, and cut wonderful capers of welcome. Between times, we scudded away to see how the dressing went on. One girl about eighteen was delightful. She dressed herself as if she did not care much about it, but could not help doing it prettily. When she took her last look at the phantom in the glass, she half smiled to it.—But *we* do not like those creatures that come into the mirror at all, your majesty. We don't understand them. They are dreadful to us.—She looked rather sad and pale, but very sweet and hopeful. So we wanted to know all about her, and soon found out that she was a distant relation and a great favourite of the gentleman of the house, an old man, in whose face benevolence was mingled with obstinacy and a deep shade of the tyrannical. We could not admire him much; but we would not make up our minds all at once: Shadows never do.

"The dinner-bell rang, and down we hurried. The children all looked happy, and we were merry. But there was one cross fellow among the servants, and didn't we plague him! and didn't we get fun out of him! When he was bringing up dishes, we lay in wait for him at every corner, and sprang upon him from the floor, and from over the bannisters, and down from the cornices. He started and stumbled and blundered so in consequence, that his fellow-servants thought he was tipsy. Once he dropped a plate, and had to pick up the pieces, and hurry away with them; and didn't we pursue him as he went! It was lucky for him his master did not see how he went on; but we took care not to let him get into any real scrape, though he was quite dazed with the dodging of the unaccountable shadows. Sometimes he thought the walls were coming down upon him, sometimes that the floor was gaping to swallow him; sometimes that he would be knocked to pieces by the hurrying to and fro, or be smothered in the black crowd.

"When the blazing plum-pudding was carried in, we made a perfect shadow-carnival about it, dancing and mumming in the blue flames, like mad demons. And how the children screamed with delight!

"The old gentleman, who was very fond of children, was laughing his heartiest laugh, when a loud knock came to the hall-door. The fair maid started, turned paler, and then red as the Christmas fire. I saw it, and flung my hands across her face. She was very glad, and I know she said in her heart, 'You kind Shadow!' which paid me well. Then I followed the rest into the hall, and found there a jolly, handsome, brown-faced sailor, evidently a son of the house. The old man received him with tears of joy. The maiden escaped in the confusion, just in time to save herself from fainting. We crowded about the lamp to hide her retreat, and nearly put it out; and the butler could not get it to burn up before she had glided into her place again, relieved to find the room so dark. The sailor only had seen her go, and now he sat down beside her, and, without a word, got hold of her hand in the gloom. When we all scattered to the walls and the corners, and the lamp blazed up again, he let her hand go.

"During the rest of dinner the old man watched the two, and saw that there was something between them, and was very angry. For he was an important man in his own estimation, and they had never consulted him. The fact was, they had never known their own minds till the sailor had gone upon his last voyage, and had learned each other's only this moment.—We found out all this by watching them, and then talking together about it afterwards.—The old gentleman saw, too, that his favourite, who was under obligation to him for loving her so much, loved his son better than him; and he grew by degrees so jealous that he overshadowed the whole table with his morose looks and short answers. That kind of shadowing is very different from ours, and the Christmas dessert grew so gloomy that we Shadows could not bear it, and were delighted when the ladies rose to go to the drawing-room. The gentlemen would not stay behind the ladies, even for the sake of the well-known wine. So the moody host, notwithstanding his hospitality, was left alone at the table in the great silent room. We followed the company up-stairs to the drawing-room, and thence to the nursery for snap-dragon; but while they were busy with this most shadowy of games, nearly all the Shadows crept downstairs again to the dining room, where the old man sat, gnawing the bone of his own selfishness. They crowded into the room, and by using every kind of expansion—blowing themselves out like soap bubbles—they succeeded in heaping up the whole room with shade upon shade. They clustered thickest about the fire and the lamp, till at last they almost drowned them in hills of darkness.

"Before they had accomplished so much, the children, tired with fun and frolic, had been put to bed. But the little girl of five years old, with whom we had been so pleased when first we arrived, could not go to sleep. She had a little room of her own; and I had watched her to bed, and now kept her awake by gambolling in the rays of the night-light. When her eyes were fixed upon me, I took the shape of her grandfather, representing him on the wall as he sat in his chair, with his head bent down and his arms hanging listlessly by his sides. And the child remembered that that was just as she had seen him last; for she had happened to peep in at the dining-room door after all the rest had gone up-stairs. 'What if he should be sitting there still,' thought she, 'all alone in the dark!' She scrambled out of bed and crept down.

"Meantime the others had made the room below so dark, that only the face and white hair of the old man could be dimly discerned in the shadowy crowd. For he had filled his own mind with shadows, which we Shadows wanted to draw out of him. Those shadows are very different from us, your majesty knows. He was thinking of all the disappointments he had had in life, and of all the ingratitude he had met with. And he thought far more of the good he had done, than the good others had got. 'After all I have done for them,' said he, with a sigh of bitterness, 'not one of them cares a straw for me. My own children will be glad when I am gone!'—At that instant he lifted up his eyes and saw, standing close by the door, a tiny figure in a long nightgown. The door behind her was shut. It was my little friend, who had crept in noiselessly. A pang of icy fear shot to the old man's heart, but it melted away as fast, for we made a lane through us for a single ray from the fire to fall on the face of the little sprite; and he thought it was a child of his own that had died when just the age of her child-niece, who now stood looking for her grandfather among the Shadows. He thought she had come out of her grave in the cold darkness to ask why her father was sitting alone on Christmas-day. And he felt he had no answer to give his little ghost, but one he would be ashamed for her to hear. But his grandchild saw him now, and walked up to him with a childish stateliness, stumbling once or twice on what seemed her long shroud. Pushing through the crowded shadows, she reached him, climbed upon his knee, laid her little long-haired head on his shoulders, and said,—'Ganpa! you gloomy? Isn't it your Kissy-Day too, ganpa?'

"A new fount of love seemed to burst from the clay of the old man's heart. He clasped the child to his bosom, and wept. Then, without a word, he rose with her in his arms, carried her up to her room, and laying her down in her bed, covered her up, kissed her sweet little mouth unconscious of reproof, and then went to the drawing-room.

"As soon as he entered, he saw the culprits in a quiet corner alone. He went up to them, took a hand of each, and joining them in both his, said, 'God bless you!' Then he turned to the rest of the company, and 'Now,' said he, 'let's have a Christmas carol.'—And well he might; for though I have paid many visits to the house, I have never seen him cross since; and I am sure that must cost him a good deal of trouble."

"We have just come from the great palace," said another, "where we knew there were many children, and where we thought to hear glad voices, and see royally merry looks. But as soon as we entered, we became aware that one mighty Shadow shrouded the whole; and that Shadow deepened and deepened, till it gathered in darkness about the reposing form of a wise prince. When we saw him, we could move no more, but clung heavily to the walls, and by our stillness added to the sorrow of the hour. And when we saw the mother of her people weeping with bowed head for the loss of him in whom she had trusted, we were seized with such a longing to be Shadows no more, but winged angels, which are the white shadows cast in heaven from the Light of Light, so as to gather around her, and hover over her with comforting, that we vanished from the walls, and found ourselves floating high above the towers of the palace, where we met the angels on their way, and knew our service was not needed."

By this time there was a glimmer of approaching to moonlight, and the king began to see several of those stranger Shadows, with human faces and eyes, moving about amongst the crowd. He knew at once that they did not belong to his dominion. They looked at him, and passed slowly, but they never made any obeisance, or gave sign of homage. And what their eyes said to him, the king only could tell. And he did not tell.

"What are those other Shadows that move through the crowd?" said he to one of his subjects near him.

The Shadow started. looked around, shivered slightly, and laid his finger on his lips. Then leading the king a little aside, and looking carefully about him once more,—

"I do not know," said he, in a low tone, "what they are. I have heard of them often, but only once did I ever see any of them before. That was when some of us one night paid a visit to a man who sat much alone, and was said to think a great deal. We saw two of those sitting in the room with him, and he was as pale as they were. We could not cross the threshold, but shivered and shook, and felt ready to melt away. Is not your majesty afraid of them too!"

But the king made no answer; and before he could speak again, the moon had climbed above the mighty pillars of the church of the Shadows, and looked in at the great window of the sky.

The shapes had all vanished; and the king, again lifting up his eyes, saw but the wall of his own chamber, on which flickered the Shadow of a Little Child. He looked down, and there, sitting on a stool by the fire, he saw one of his own little ones, waiting to say good-night to his father, and go to bed early, but he might rise early too, and be very good and happy all Christmas-day.

And Ralph Rinkelmann rejoiced that he was a man, and not a Shadow.

But as the Shadows vanished they left the sense of song in the king's brain. And the words of their song must have been something like these:—

> "Shadows, Shadows, Shadows all!
> Shadow birth and funeral!
> Shadow moons gleam overhead;
> Over shadow-graves we tread.
> Shadow-hope lives, grows, and dies.

"*Shadow-love from shadow-eyes*
    Shadow-ward entices on
    To shadow-words on shadow-stone,
    Closing up the shadow-shadow-wail.

"*Shadow-man, thou art a gloom*
    Cast upon a shadow-tomb
    Through the endless shadow-air,
    From the Shadow sitting there,
    On a moveless shadow-throne,
    Glooming through the ages gone;
    North and south, and in and out,
    East and west, and all about,
    Flinging Shadows everywhere
    On the shadow-painted air,
    Shadow-man, thou hast no story;
    Nothing but a shadow-glory."

But Ralph Rinkelmann said to himself,—

"They are but Shadows that sing thus; for a Shadow can see but Shadows. A man sees a man where a Shadow sees only a Shadow."

And he was comforted in himself.

Birth, Dreaming, Death

In a little room, scantily furnished, lighted, not from the window, for it was dark without, and the shutters were closed, but from the peaked flame of a small clear-burning lamp, sat a young man, with his back to the lamp and his face to the fire. No book or paper on the table indicated labour just forsaken; nor could one tell from his eyes, in which the light had all retreated inwards, whether his consciousness was absorbed in thought, or reverie only. The window curtains, which scarcely concealed the shutters, were of coarse texture, but of brilliant scarlet,—for he loved bright colours; and the faint reflection they threw on his pale face, made it look more delicate than it would have seemed in pure daylight. Two or three bookshelves, suspended by cords from a nail in the wall, contained a collection of books, poverty-stricken as to numbers, with but a few to fill up the chronological gap between the Greek New Testament and stray volumes of the poets of the present century. But his love for the souls of the individual books was the stronger that there was no possibility of its degenerating into avarice for the bodies or outsides whose aggregate constitutes the piece of house-furniture called a library.

Some years before, the young man (my story is so short, and calls in so few personages, that I need not give him a name) had aspired, under the influence of religious and sympathetic feeling, to be a clergyman; but Providence, either in the form of poverty, or of theological difficulty, had prevented his prosecuting his studies to that end. And now he was *only* a village schoolmaster; but is it not better to be a teacher *of* babes than a preacher *to* men, at any time; not to speak of those troublesome times of transition, wherein a difference of degree must so often assume the appearance of a difference of kind? That man is more happy—I will not say more blessed—who, loving boys and girls, is loved and revered by them, than he who, ministering unto men and women, is compelled to pour his words into the filter of religious suspicion, whence the water is allowed to pass away unheeded, and only the residuum is retained for the analysis of ignorant party-spirit.

He had married a simple village girl, in whose eyes he was nobler than the noblest—to whom he was the mirror, in which the real forms of all things around were reflected. Who dares pity my poor village schoolmaster? I fling his pity away. Had he not found in her love the verdict of God, that he was worth loving? Did he not in her possess the

eternal and unchangeable? Were not her eyes openings through which
he looked into the great depths that could not be measured or
represented? She was his public, his society, his critic. He found in her
the heaven of his rest. God gave unto him immortality, and he was glad.
For his ambition, it had died of its own mortality. He read the words of
Jesus, and the words of great prophets whom he has sent; and learned
that the wind-tossed anemone is a word of God as real and true as the
unbending oak beneath which it grows—that reality is an absolute
existence precluding degrees. If his mind was, as his room, scantily
furnished, it was yet lofty; if his light was small, it was brilliant. God
lived, and he lived. Perhaps the highest moral height which a man can
reach, and at the same time most difficult of attainment, is the willing to
be *nothing* relatively, so that he attain that positive excellence which the
original conditions of his being render not merely possible, but
imperative. It is nothing to a man to be greater or less than another; to
be esteemed or otherwise by the public or private world in which he
moves. Does he, or does he not, behold and love and live the
unchangeable, the essential, the divine? This he can only do according as
God has made him. He can hold and understand God in the least degree,
as well as in the greatest, only by the godlike within him; and he that
loves thus the good and great has no room, no thought, no necessity
for comparison and difference. The truth satisfies him. He lives in its
absoluteness. God makes the glow-worm as well as the star; the light in
both is divine. If mine be an earth-star to gladden the wayside, I must
cultivate humbling and rejoicingly its green earth-glow, and not seek to
blanch it to the whiteness of the stars that lie in the fields of blue. For to
deny God in my being is to cease to behold him in any. God and man
can meet only by the man's becoming that which God meant him to be.
Then he enters into the house of life, which is greater than the house of
fame. It is better to be a child in a green field than a knight of many
orders in a state ceremonial.

All night long he had sat there, and morning was drawing nigh. He
has not heard the busy wind all night, heaping up snow against the
house, which will make him start at the ghostly face of the world when
at length he opens the shutters, and it stares upon him so white. For up
in a little room above, white-curtained, like the great earth without,
there has been a storm, too, half the night—and moanings and
prayers—and some forbidden tears; but now, at length, it is over; and
through the portals of two mouths instead of one, flows and ebbs the
tide of the great air-sea which feeds the life of man. With the sorrow of

the mother; our very being is redeemed from nothingness with the pains of a death of which we know nothing.

An hour has gone by since the watcher below has been delivered from the fear and doubt that held him. He has seen the mother and the child—the first she has given to life and him, and has returned to his only room, quiet and glad.

But not long does he sit thus before thought of doubt awoke in his mind. He remembered his scanty income, and the somewhat feeble health of his wife. One or two small debts he had contracted seemed absolutely to press on his bosom; and the newborn child—"oh! how doubly welcome, he thought, if I were but half as rich again as I am!"—brought with it, as its own love, so its own care. The dogs of need, that so often hunt us up to heaven, seemed hard upon his heels; and he prayed to God with fervour; and as he prayed he fell asleep in his chair, and as he slept he dreamed. The fire and the lamp burned on as before, but they no rays into his soul; yet now, for the first time, he seemed to become aware of the storm without; for his dream was as follows:

He lay in his bed, and listened to the howling of the wintry wind. He trembled at the thought of the pitiless cold, and turned to sleep again, when he thought he heard a feeble knocking at the door. He rose in haste, and went down with a light. As he opened the door, the wind, entering with a gust of frosty particles, blew out his candle; but he found it unnecessary, for the grey dawn had come. Looking out he saw nothing at first; but a second look, turned downwards, showed him a little half-frozen child, who looked quietly, but beseechingly, in his face. His hair was filled with drifted snow, and his little hands and cheeks were blue with cold. The heart of the schoolmaster swelled to bursting with the spring-flood of love and pity that rose up within it. He lifted the child to his bosom, and carried him into the house, where, in the dream's incongruity, he found a fire blazing in the room in which he now slept. The child said never a word. He set him by the fire, and made haste to get hot water, and put him in a warm bath. He never doubted that this was a stray orphan who had wandered to him for protection, and he felt that he could not part with him again; even though the train of his previous troubles and doubts once more passed through the mind of the dreamer, and there seemed no answer to his perplexities for the lack of that cheap thing, gold—yea, silver. But when he had undressed and bathed the little orphan, and having dried him on his knees, set him down to reach something warm to wrap him in, the boy suddenly looked up in his face, as if revived, and said with a heavenly smile, "I am the child Jesus." "The child Jesus!" said the dreamer, astonished. "Thou art like any other child." "No, do not say so," returned the boy; "but say *Any other child is like me.*" And the child and the dream slowly faded away; and he awoke with these words sounding in his heart—"Whosoever shall receive one of such children in my name, receiveth me; and whosever shall receive me, receiveth not me, but him that sent me." It was the voice of God saying to him, "Thou wouldst receive the child of the cold waste into the warm, human house, as the door by which it enters God's house, it's home. If better could be done for it, or for thee, would I have sent it hither? Through thy love, my little one must learn my love and be blessed. And thou shalt not keep it without thy reward. For thy necessities—in thy little house, is there not yet room? in thy barrel, is there not yet meal? and thy purse is not empty quite. Thou canst not eat more than a mouthful at once. I have made thee so. Is it any trouble to me to take care of thee? Only I prefer to feed thee from my own hand, and not from thy store." And the schoolmaster sprang up in joy, ran up stairs, kissed his wife, and clasped the baby in his arms in the name of the child Jesus. And in that embrace, he knew that he received God to his heart. Soon, with a tender, beaming face, he was wading through the snow to the school-house, where he spent a happy day amidst the rosy faces and bright eyes of his boys and girls. These, likewise, he loved the more dearly and joyfully for that dream, and those words in his heart, so that, amidst their child-faces, (all going well with them, as not infrequently happened in his schoolroom), he felt as if all the elements of Paradise were gathered around him, and knew that he was God's child, doing God's work.

But while that dream was passing through the soul of the husband, another visited the wife, as she lay in the faintness and trembling joy of the new motherhood. For although she that has been mother before, is not less a new mother to the new child, her former relation not covering with its wings the fresh bird in the nest of her bosom, yet there must be a peculiar delight in the thought and feelings that come with the first-born.—As she lay half in a sleep, half in a faint, with the vapours of a gentle delirium floating to her brain, without losing the sense of existence she lost the consciousness of its form, and thought she lay, not a young mother in her bed, but a nosegay of wild flowers in a basket, crushed, flattened and half-withered. With her in the basket lay other bunches of flowers, whose odours, some rare as well as rich, revealed to her the sad contrast in which she was placed. Beside her lay a cluster of delicately curved, faintly tinged, tea-scented roses; while she was only blue hyacinth bells, pale primroses, amethyst anemones, closed blood-coloured daisies, purple violets, and one sweet-scented, pure white orchid. The basket lay on the counter of a well-known shop in the little village, waiting for purchasers. By and by her own husband entered the shop, and approached the basket to choose a nosegay. "Ah!" thought she, "will he choose me? How dreadful if he should not, and I should be left lying here, while he takes another! But how should he choose me? They are all so beautiful; and even my scent is nearly gone. And he cannot know that it is I lying here. Alas! alas!" But as she thought thus, she felt his hand clasp her, heard the ransom-money fall, and felt that she was pressed to his face and lips, as he passed from the shop. He *had* chosen her; he *had* known her. She opened her eyes; her husband's kiss had awakened her. She did not speak, but looked up thankfully in his eyes, as if he had, in fact, like one of the old knights, delivered her from the transformation of some evil magic, by the counter-enchantment of a kiss, and restored her from a half-withered nosegay to a woman, a wife, a mother. The dream comforted her much, for she had often feared that she, the simple, so-called uneducated girl, could not be enough for the great schoolmaster. But soon her thoughts flowed into another channel; the tears rose in her eyes, shining clear from beneath a stream that was not of sorrow; and it was only weakness that kept her from uttering audible words like these:—"Father in heaven, shall I trust my husband's love, and doubt thine? Wilt thou meet less richly the fearing hope of thy child's heart, than he in my dream met the longing of his wife's? He was perfected in my eyes by the love he bore me—shall I find thee less complete? Here I lie on thy world, faint, and crushed, and withered; and my soul often seems as if it had lost all the odours that should float up in the sweet-smelling savour of thankfulness and love to thee. But thou hast only to take me, only to choose me, only to clasp me to thy bosom, and I shall be a beautiful singing angel, singing to God, and comforting my husband while I sing. Father, take me, possess me, fill me!"

So she lay patiently waiting for the summer-time of restored strength that drew slowly nigh. With her husband and her child near her, in her soul, and God everywhere, there was for her no death, and no hurt. When she said to herself, "How rich I am!" it was with the riches that pass not away—the riches of the Son of man; for in her treasures, the human and divine were blended—were one.

But there was a hard trial in store for them. They had learned to receive what the Father sent: they had now to learn that what he gave he gave eternally, after his own being—his own glory. For ere the mother awoke from her first sleep, the baby, like a frolicsome child-angel, that but tapped at his mother's window and fled,—the baby died; died while the mother slept away the pangs of birth; died while the father was teaching other babes out of the joy of his new fatherhood.

When the mother woke, she lay still in her joy—the joy of a doubled life; and knew not that death had been there, and had left behind only the little human coffin.

"Nurse, bring me the baby," she said at last. "I want to see it."

But the nurse pretended not to hear.

"I want to nurse it. Bring it."

She had not yet learned to say *him*; for it was her first baby.

But the nurse went out of the room and remained some minutes away. When she returned, the mother spoke more absolutely, and the nurse was compelled to reply—at last.

"Nurse, do bring me the baby; I am quite able to nurse it now."

"Not yet, if you please, ma'am. Really you must rest a while first. Do try to go to sleep."

The nurse spoke steadily, and looked her, too, straight in the face; and there was a constraint in her voice, a determination to be calm, that at once roused the suspicion of the mother; for though her first-born was dead, and she had given birth to what was now, as far as the eye could reach, the waxen image of a son, a child had come from God, and had departed to him again; and she *was* his mother.

And the fear fell upon her heart that it might be as it was; and, looking at her attendant with a face blanched yet more with fear than with suffering, she said,

"Nurse, is the baby——?"

She could not say *dead*; for to utter the word would be at once to make it possible that the only fruit of her labour had been pain and sorrow.

But the nurse saw that further concealment was impossible; and, without another word, went and fetched the husband, who, with face as pale as the mother's, brought the baby, dressed in its white clothes, and laid it by its mother's side, where it lay too still.

"Oh, ma'am, do not take on so," said the nurse, as she saw the face of the mother grow like the face of the child, as if she were about to rush after him into the dark.

But she was not "taking on" at all. She only felt that pain at her heart, which is the farewell-kiss of a long-cherished joy. Though cast out of paradise into a world that looked very dull and weary, yet, used to suffering, and always claiming from God the consolation it needed, and satisfied with that, she was able, presently, to look up in her husband's face, and try to reassure him of her well-being by a dreary smile.

"Leave the baby," she said; and they left it where it was. Long and earnestly she gazed on the perfect tiny features of the little alabaster countenance, and tried to feel that this was the child she had been so long waiting for. As she looked, she fancied she heard it breathe, and she thought—"What if it should be only asleep!" but, alas! the eyes wandered over the little face, a look of her husband dawned unexpectedly upon it; and, as if the wife's heart awoke the mother's, she cried out, "Baby! baby!" and burst into tears, during which weeping she fell asleep.

When she awoke, she found the babe had been removed while she slept. But the unsatisfied heart of the mother longed to look again on the form of the child; and again, though with remonstrance from the nurse, it was laid beside her. All day and all night long, it remained by her side, like a little frozen thing that wandered from its home, and now lay dead by the door.

Next morning the nurse protested that she must part with it, for it made her fret; but she knew it quieted her, and she would rather keep her little lifeless babe. At length the nurse appealed to the father; and the mother feared he would think it necessary to remove it; but to her joy and gratitude he said, "No; no, let her keep it as long as she likes." And she loved her husband the more for that; for he understood her.

Then she had the cradle brought near her bed, all ready as it was for a live child that had open eyes, and therefore needed sleep—needed the lids of the brain to close, when it was filled full of the strange colours and forms of the new world. But this one needed no cradle, for it slept on. It needed, instead of the little curtains to darken it to sleep, a great sunlight to wake it from the darkness, and the ever-satisfied rest. Yet she laid it in the cradle, which she had set near her, where she could see, with the little hand and arm laid out on the white coverlet. If she could only keep it so! Could not something be done, if not to awake it, yet to turn it to stone, and let it remain so for ever? No, the body must go back to its Father—the Maker. And as it lay in the white cradle, a white coffin was being made for it. And the mother thought: "I wonder which trees are growing coffins for my husband and me."

But ere the child, that had the prayer of Job in his grief, and had died from its mother's womb, was carried away to be buried, the mother prayed over it this prayer:—"O God, if thou wilt not let me be a mother, I have one refuge: I will go back and be a child: I will be thy child more than ever. My mother-heart will find relief in childhood towards its Father. For is it not the same nature that makes the true mother and the true child? Is it not the same thought blossoming upward and blossoming downward? So there is God the Father and God the Son. Thou wilt keep my little son for me. He has gone home to be nursed for me. And when I grow well, I will be more simple, and truthful, and joyful in thy sight. And now thou art taking away my child, my plaything from me. But I think how pleased I should be, if I had a daughter, and she loved me so well that she only smiled when I took her plaything from her. Oh! I will not disappoint thee—thou shalt have thy joy. Here I am, do with me what thou wilt; I will only smile."

And how fared the heart of the father? At first, in the bitterness of his grief, he called the loss of his child a punishment for his doubt and unbelief; and the feeling of punishment made the stroke more keen, and the heart less willing to endure it. But the better thoughts woke within him ere long.

The old woman who swept out his schoolroom, came in the evening to inquire after the mistress, and to offer her condolences on the loss of the baby. She came likewise to tell the news, that a certain old man of little respectability had departed at last, unregretted by a single soul in the village but herself, who had been his nurse through his last tedious illness.

The schoolmaster thought with himself:

"Can that soiled and withered leaf of a man, and my little snow-flake of a baby, have gone the same road? Will they meet by the way? Can they talk about the same thing—anything? They must part on the borders of the shining land, and they could hardly speak by the way."

"He will live four-and-twenty hours, nurse," the doctor had said.

"No, doctor; he will die to-night," the nurse had replied; during which whispered dialogue, the patient had lain breathing quietly, for the last of suffering was nearly over.

He was at the close of an ill-spent life, not so much selfishly towards others as indulgently towards himself. He had failed of true joy by trying often and perseveringly to create a false one; and now, about to knock at the gate of the other world, he bore with him no burden of the good things of this; and one might be tempted to say of him, that it were better he had not been born. The great majestic mystery lay before him—but when would he see its majesty?

He was dying thus, because he had tried to live as Nature said he should not live; and he had taken his own wages—for the law of the Maker is the necessity of his creature. His own children had forsaken him, for they were not perfect as their Father in heaven, who maketh his sun to shine on the evil and on the good. Instead of doubling their care as need doubled, they had thought of the disgrace he had brought upon them, and not of the duty they owed him; and now, left to die alone for them, he was waited on by his hired nurse, who, familiar with death-beds, knew better than the doctor, knew that he could live only a few hours.

Stooping to his ear, she had told him, as gently as she could,—for she thought she ought not to conceal it—that he must die that night. He had lain silent for a few moments; then had called her, and, with broken and failing voice, had said, "Nurse, you are the only friend I have; give me one kiss before I die." And the woman-heart had answered the prayer.

"And," said the old woman, "he put his arms round my neck, and gave me a long, such a long kiss! and then he turned his face away, and never spoke again."

So, with the last unction of a woman's kiss, with this baptism for the dead, he had departed.

"Poor old man! he had not quite destroyed his heart yet," thought the schoolmaster. "Surely it was the child-nature that woke in him at the last, when the only thing left for his soul to desire, the only thing he could think of as a preparation for the dread something, was a kiss. Strange conjunction, yet simple and natural! Eternity—a kiss. Kiss me, for I am going to the Unknown!—Poor old man," the schoolmaster went on his thoughts. "I hope my baby has met him, and put his tiny hand in the poor old shaking hand, and so led him across the borders into the shining land, and up to where Jesus sits, and said to the Lord: 'Lord, forgive this old man, for he knew not what he did.' And I trust the Lord has forgiven him."

And then the bereaved father fell on his knees, and cried out:

"Lord, thou hast not punished me. Thou wouldst not punish for a passing thought of troubled unbelief, with which I strove. Lord, take my child and his mother and me, and do what thou wilt with us. I know thou givest not, to take again."

And ere the schoolmaster could call his Protestantism to his aid, he had ended his prayer with the cry:

"And O God! have mercy on the poor old man, and lay not his sins to his charge."

For, though a woman's kiss may comfort a man to eternity, it is not all he needs. And the thought of his lost child had made the soul of the father compassionate.

My Uncle Peter

I will tell you the story of my Uncle Peter, who was born on Christmas-day. He was very anxious to die on Christmas-day as well; but I must confess that was rather ambitious in Uncle Peter. Shakespeare is said to have been born on St. George's-day, and there is some ground for believing that he died on St. George's-day. He thus fulfilled a cycle. But we cannot expect that of any but great men, and Uncle Peter was not a great man, though I think that I shall be able to show that he was a good man. The only pieces of selfishness I ever discovered in him were, his self-gratulation at having been born on Christmas-day, and the ambition with regard to his death, which I have just recorded; and that this little selfishness was not a kind to be very injurious to his fellowmen, I think I shall be able to show as well.

The first remembrance that I have of him, is his taking me one Christmas-eve to the largest toy-shop in London, and telling me to choose any toy whatever that I pleased. He little knew the agony of choice into which this request of his,—for it was put to me as a request, in the most polite, loving manner,—threw his astonished nephew. If a general right of choice from the treasures of the whole world had been unanimously voted me, it could hardly have cast me into greater perplexity. I wandered about, staring like a distracted ghost at the "wealth of Ormus and of Ind," displayed about me. Uncle Peter followed me with perfect patience; nay, I believe, with a delight that equaled my perplexity, for, every now and then when I looked round to him with a silent appeal for sympathy in the distressing dilemma into which he had thrown me, I found him rubbing his hands and spiritually chuckling over his victim. Nor would he volunteer the least assistance to save me from the dire consequences of too much liberty. How long I was in making up my mind I cannot tell; but as I look back upon this splendour of my childhood, I feel as if I must have wandered for weeks through interminable forest-alleys of toy-bearing trees. As often as I read the story of Aladdin—and I read it now and then still, for I have children about, and their books about—the subterranean orchard of jewels always brings me back to my inward vision of the inexhaustible riches of the toy-shop to which Uncle Peter took me that Christmas-eve. As soon as, in despair of choosing well, I had made a desperate plunge at my decision, my Uncle Peter, as if to forestall any supervention of repentance, began buying like a maniac, giving me everything that took his fancy or mine, till we and our toys nearly filled the cab which he called to take us home.

Uncle Peter was a little round man, not *very* fat, resembling both in limbs and features an overgrown baby. And I believe the resemblance was not merely an external one; for, though his intellect was quite up to par, he retained a degree of simplicity of character and of tastes that was not childlike only, but bordered, sometimes, upon the childish. To look at him, you could not have fancied a face or a figure with less of the romantic about them; yet I believe that the whole region of his brain was held in fee-simple, whatever that may mean, by a race of fairy architects, who built aerial castles therein, regardless of expense. His imagination was the most distinguishing feature of his character. And to hear him defend any of his extravagancies, it would appear that he considered himself especially privileged in that respect. "Ah, my dear," he would say to my mother when she expostulated with him on making some present far beyond the small means he at that time possessed, "ah, my dear, you see I was born on Christmas-day." Many a time he would come in from town, where he was a clerk in a merchant's office, with the water running out of his boots, and his umbrella carefully tucked under his arm; and we would know very well that he had given the last coppers he had, for his omnibus home, to some beggar or crossing-sweeper, and had then been so delighted with the pleasure he had given, that he forgot to make the best of it by putting up his umbrella. Home he would trudge, in his worn suit of black, with his steel watch-chain and bunch of ancestral seals swinging and ringing from his fob, and the rain running into his trousers pockets, to the great endangerment of the health of his cherished old silver watch, which never went wrong because it was put right every day by St. Paul's. He was quite poor then, as I have said. I do not think he had more than a hundred pounds a-year, and he must have been five and thirty. I suppose his employers showed their care for the morals of their clerks, by never allowing them any margin to mis-spend. But Uncle Peter lived in constant hope and expectation of some unexampled good luck befalling him: "For," he said, "I was born on Christmas-day."

He was never married. When people used to jest with him about being an old bachleor, he used to smile, for anything would make him smile; but I was a very little boy indeed when I began to observe that the smile on such occasions was mingled with sadness, and Uncle Peter's face looked very much as if he was going to cry. But he never said anything on the subject, and not even my mother knew if he had any love-story or not. I have often wondered whether his goodness might not come in part from his having lost some one very dear to him, and having his life on earth purified by the thoughts of her life in heaven. But I never found out. After his death—for he did die, though not on Christmas-day—I found a lock of hair folded in paper with a date on it—that was all—in a secret drawer of his old desk. The date was far earlier than my first recollections of him. I reverentially burnt it with fire.

He lived in lodgings by himself not far from our house; and, when not with us, was pretty sure to be found seated in his easy-chair, for he was fond of simple comforts, beside a good fire, reading by the light of one candle. He had his tea always as soon as he came home, and some buttered toast or hot muffin, of which he was sure to make me eat three-quarters if I chanced to drop in upon him at the right hour, which, I am ashamed to say, I not unfrequently did. He dared not order another, as I soon discovered. Yet, I fear, that did not abate my appetite for what there was. You see, I was never so good as Uncle Peter. When he had finished his tea, he turned his chair to the fire, and read—what do you think? Sensible Travels and Discoveries, or Political Economy, or Popular Geology? No: Fairy Tales, as many as he could lay hold of; and when they failed him, Romances or Novels. Almost anything in this way would do that was not bad. I believe he had read every word of Richardson's novels, and most of Fielding's and De Foe's. But once I saw him throw a volume into the fire, which he had been fidgeting over for a while. I was just finishing a sum I had brought across to him to help me with. I looked up, and saw the volume in the fire. The heat made it writhe open, and I saw the aithor's name, and that was *Sterne*. He had brought it at a book-stall as he came home. He sat awhile, and then got up and took down his Bible, and began reading a chapter in the New Testament, as if for an antidote to the book he had destroyed.

But Uncle Peter's luck came at last—at least, he thought it did, when he received a lawyer's letter announcing the *demise* of a cousin of whom he had heard little for a great many years, although they had been warm friends while at school together. This cousin had been brought up to some trade in the wood line—had been a cooper or a carpenter, and had somehow or other got landed in India, and, though not in the Company's service, had contrived in one way or the another to amass what might be called a large fortune in any rank of life. I am afraid to mention the amount of it, lest it should throw discredit on my story. The whole of this fortune he left to Uncle Peter, for he had no nearer relation, and had always remembered him with affection.

I happened to be seated beside my uncle when the lawyer's letter arrived. He was reading "Peter Wilkins." He laid down the book with reluctance, thinking the envelope contained some advertisement of slaty coal for his kitchen-fire, or cottony silk for girls' dresses. Fancy my surprise when my uncle jumped up on his chair, and thence on the table, upon which he commenced a sort of demoniac hornpipe. But that sober article of furniture declined giving its support to such proceedings for a single moment, and fell with an awful crash to the floor. My uncle was dancing amidst its ruin like Nero in blazing Rome, when he was reduced to an awful sense of impropriety by the entrance of his landlady. I was sitting in open-mouthed astonishment at my uncle's extravagance, when he suddenly dropped into his chair, like a lark into its nest, leaving heaven silent. But silence did not reign long.

"*Well!* Mr. Belper," began his landlady, in a tone difficult of description as it is easy of conception, for her fists had already planted themselves in her own opposing sides. But, to my astonishment, my uncle was not in the least awed, although I am sure, however much he tried to hide it, that I have often seen him tremble in his shoes at the distant roar of this tigress. But it is wonderful how much courage a pocketful of sovereigns will give. It is far better for rousing the pluck of a man than any number of bottles of wine in his head. What a brave thing a whole fortune must be then!

"Take that rickety old thing away," said my uncle.

"Rickety, Mr. Belper! I'm astonished to hear a decent gentleman like you slander the very table as you've eaten off the last—"

"We won't be precise to a year, ma'am," interrupted my uncle.

"And if you will have little scapegraces of neveys into my house to break the furniture, why, them as breaks, pays, Mr. Belper."

"Very well. Of course I will pay for it. I broke it myself, ma'am; and if you don't get out of my room, I'll—"

"Uncle Peter jumped up once more, and made for the heap of ruins in the middle of the floor. The landlady vanished in a moment, and my uncle threw himself again into his chair, and absolutely roared with laughter.

"Shan't we have rare fun, Charlie, my boy?" said he at last, and went off into another fit of laughter.

"Why, uncle, what is the matter with you?" I managed to say, in utter bewilderment.

"Nothing but luck, Charlie. It's gone to my head. I'm not used to it, Charlie, that's all. I'll come all right by-and-by. Bless you, my boy!"

What do you think was the first thing my uncle did to relieve himself of the awful accession of power which had just befallen him? The following morning he gathered together every sixpence he had in the house, and went out of one grocer's shop into another, and out of one baker's shop into another, until he had changed the whole into threepenny pieces. Then he walked to town, as usual, to business. But one or two of his friends who were walking the same way, and followed behind him, could not think what Mr. Belper was about. Every crossing that he came to he made use of to cross to the other side. He crossed and recrossed the same street twenty times, they said. But at length they observed, that, with a legerdemain worthy of a professor, he slipped something into every sweeper's hand as he passed him. It was one of the threepenny pieces. When he walked home in the evening, he had nothing to give, and besides went through one of the wet experiences to which I have alluded. To add to his discomfort, he found, when he got home, that his tobacco-jar was quite empty, so that he was forced to put on his wet shoes again—for he never, to the end of his days, had more than one pair at a time—in order to come across to my mother to borrow sixpence. Before the legacy was paid to him, he went through a good many of the tortures which result from being "a king and no king." The inward consciousness and outward possibility did not in the least correspond. At length, after much manoeuvring with the lawyers, who seemed to sympathize with the departed cousin in this, that they too would prefer keeping the money till death parted them, he succeeded in getting a thousand pounds of it on Christmas-eve.

"NOW!" said Uncle Peter, in enormous capitals.—That night a thundering knock came to our door. We were sitting in our little dining room—father, and mother, and seven children of us—talking about what we should do next day. The door opened, and in came the most grotesque figure you could imagine. It was seven feet high at least, without any head, a mere walking tree-stump, as far as shape went, only it looked soft. The little ones were terrified, but not the bigger ones of us; for from top to toe (if it had a toe) it was covered with toys of every conceivable description, fastened on to it somehow or other. It was a perfect treasure-cave of Ali Baba turned inside out. We shrieked with delight. The figure stood perfectly still, and we gathered round it in a group to have a nearer view of the wonder. We then discovered that there were tickets on all the articles, which we supposed at first to record the price of each. But, upon still closer examination, we discovered that every one of the tickets had one or other of our names upon it. This caused a fresh explosion of joy. Nor was it the children only that we thus remembered. A little box bore my mother's name. When she opened it, we saw a real gold watch and chain, and seals and dangles of every sort, of useful and useless kind; and my mother's initials were on the back of the watch. My father had a silver flute, and to the music of it we had such a dance! the strange figure, now considerable lighter, joining in it without uttering a word. During the dance one of my sisters, a very sharp-eyed little puss, espied about half way up the monster two bright eyes looking out of a shadowy depth of something like the skirts of a great coat. She peeped and peeped; and at length, with a perfect scream of exultation, cried out, "It's Uncle Peter! It's Uncle Peter!" The music ceased; the dance was forgotten; we flew upon him like a pack of hungry wolves; we tore him to the ground; despoiled him of coats and plaids, and elevating sticks; and discovered the kernel of the beneficent monster in the person of real Uncle Peter; which, after all, was the best present he could have brought us on Christmas-eve, for we had been very dull for want of him, and had been wondering why he did not come.

But Uncle Peter had great plans for his birthday, and for the carrying out of them he took me into his confidence,—I being now a lad of fifteen, and partaking sufficiently of my uncle's nature to enjoy at least the fun of his benevolence. He had been for some time perfecting his information about a few of the families in the neighbourhood; for he was a bit of a gossip, and did not turn his landlady out when she came to expostulate about the table. But she knew her lodger well enough never to dare to bring him any scandal. From her he had learned that a certain artist in the neighbourhood was very poor. He made inquiry about him where he thought he could hear more, and finding that he was steady and hard-working (Uncle Peter never cared to inquire whether he had genius or not; it was enough to him that the poor fellow's pictures did not sell), resolves that he should have a more pleasant Christmas than he expected. One other chief outlet for his brotherly love, in the present instance, was a dissenting minister and his wife, who had a large family of little children. They lived in the same street as himself. Uncle Peter was an unwavering adherent to the Church of England, but he would have felt himself a dissenter at once if he had excommunicated any one by withdrawing his sympathies from him. He knew that this minister was a thoroughly good man, and he had even gone to hear him preach once or twice. He knew too that his congregation was not the more liberal to him that he was liberal to all men. So he resolved that he would act the part of one of the black angels that brought bread and meat to Elijah in the wilderness. Uncle Peter would never have pretended to rank higher than one of the foresaid ravens.

A great part of the forenoon of Christmas-day was spent by my uncle and me in preparations. The presents he had planned were many, but I will only mention two or three of them in particular. For the minister and his family he got a small bottle with a large mouth. This he filled as full of sovereigns as it would hold; labelled it outside, *Pickled Mushrooms*; "for doesn't it grow in the earth without any seed?" said he; and then wrapped it up like a grocer's parcel. For the artist, he took a large shell from his chimney-piece; folded a fifty-pound note in a bit of paper, which he tied up with a green ribbon; inserted the paper in the jaws of the shell, so that the ends of ribbon should hang out; folded it up in paper and sealed it; wrote outside, *Enquire within*; enclosed the whole in a tin box and directed it, *With Christmas day's compliments*; "for wasn't I born on Christmas-day?" concluded Uncle Peter for the twentieth time that forenoon. Then there were a dozen or two of the best port he could get, for a lady who had just had a baby, and whose husband and his income he knew from business relations. Nor were the children forgotten. Every house in his street and ours in which he knew there were little ones, had a parcel of toys and sweet things prepared for it.

As soon as the afternoon grew dusky, we set out with as many parcels as we could carry. A slight disguise secured me from discovery, my duty being to leave the parcels at the different houses. In the case of the more valuable of them, my duty was to ask for the master or mistress, and see the packet in safe hands. In this I was successful in every instance. It must have been a great relief to my uncle when the number of parcels were sufficiently diminished to restore to him the use of his hands, for to him they were necessary for rubbing as a tail is to a dog for wagging—in both cases for electrical reasons, no doubt. He dropped several parcels in the vain attempt to hold them and perform the usual frictional movement notwithstanding; so he was compelled instead to go through a kind of solemn pace, which got more and more rapid as the parcels decreased in number, till it became at last, in its wild movements, something like a Highlander's sword-dance. We had to go home several times for more, keeping the best till last. When Uncle Peter saw me give the "pickled mushrooms" into the hands of the lady of the house, he uttered a kind of laugh, strangled into a crow, which startled the good lady, who was evidently rather alarmed at the weight of the small parcel, for she said, with a scared look:—

"It's not gunpowder, is it?"

"No," I said; "I think it's shot."

"Shot!" said she, looking even more alarmed. "Don't you think you had better take it back again?"

She held out the parcel to me, and made as if she would shut the door.

"Why, ma'am," I answered, "you would not have me taken up for stealing it?"

It was a foolish reply; but it answered the purpose if not the question. She kept the parcel and shut the door. When I looked round I saw my uncle going through a regular series of convolutions, corresponding exactly to the bodily contortions he must have executed at school every time he received a course of what they call *palmies* in Scotland; if, indeed, Uncle Peter was ever even suspected of improper behaviour at school. It consisted first of a dance, then a double-up; then another dance, then another double-up, and so on.

"Some stupid hoax, I suppose!" said the artist, as I put the parcel into his hands. He looked gloomy enough, poor fellow.

"Don't be too sure of that, if you please, sir" said I, and vanished.

Everything was a good joke to my uncle all evening.

"Charlie," said he, "I never had such a birthday in my life before; but, please God, now I've begun, this will not be the last of the sort. But, you young rascal, if you split, why, I'll thrash the life out of you. No, I won't—" here my uncle assumed a dignified attitude, and concluded with mock solemnity—"No, I won't. I will cut you off with a shilling."

This was a *crescendo* passage, ending in a howl; upon which he commenced once more an edition of the Highland fling, with impromptu variations.

When the parcels were delivered, we walked home together to my uncle's lodgings, where he gave me a glass of wine and a sovereign for my trouble. I believe I felt as rich as any of them.

But now I must tell you the romance of my uncle's life. I do not mean the suspected hidden romance, for no one knew—except, indeed a dead one knew all about it. It was a later romance, which, however, nearly cost him his life once.

One Christmas-eve we had been occupied, as usual, with the presents of the following Christmas-day, and—will you believe it?—in the same lodgings, too, for my uncle was a thorough Tory in his hatred of change. Indeed, although two years had passed, and he had had the whole of his property at his disposal since the legal term of one year, he still continued to draw his salary of £100 of Messrs. Buff and Codgers. One Christmas-eve, I say, I was helping him to make up parcels, when, from a sudden impulse, I said to him—

"How good you are, uncle!"

"Ha! ha! ha!" laughed he; "that's the best joke of all. Good, my boy! Ha! ha! ha! Why, Charlie, you don't fancy I care one atom for all these people, do you? I do it all to please myself. Ha! ha! ha! That *is* a joke. Good, indeed! Ha! ha! ha!"

I am happy to say I was an old enough bird not to be caught with this metaphysical chaff. But my uncle's face grew suddenly very grave, even sad in its expression; and after a pause he resumed, but this time without laughing:—

"Good, Charlie! Why, I'm no use to anybody."

"You do me good, anyhow, uncle," I answered. "If I'm not a better man for having you for an uncle, why I should be a great deal the worse, that's all."

"Why, there it is!" rejoined my uncle; "I don't know whether I do good or harm. But for you, Charlie, you're a good boy, and don't want any good done to you. It would break my heart, Charlie, if I thought you weren't a good boy."

He always called me boy after I was a grown man. But then I believe he always felt like a boy himself, and quite forgot that we were uncle and nephew.

I was silent, and he resumed,—

"I wish I could be of real, unmistakeable use to anyone! But I fear I am not good enough to have that honour done me."

Next morning,—that was Christmas-day,—he went out for a walk alone, apparently oppressed with the thought with which the serious part of our conversation on the preceding evening had closed. Of course nothing less than a threepenny piece would do for a crossing-sweeper on Christmas-day; but one tiny little girl touched his heart so that the usual coin was doubled. Still this did not relieve the heart of the giver sufficiently; for the child looked up in his face in a way, whatever the way was, that made his heart ache. So he gave her a shilling. But he felt no better after that.—I am following his own account of feelings and circumstances.

"This won't do," said Uncle Peter to himself. "What is your name?" said Uncle Peter to the little girl.

"Little Christmas," she answered.

"Little Christmas!" exclaimed Peter. "I see why that wouldn't do now. What do you mean?"

"Little Christmas, sir; please, sir."

"Who calls you that?"

"Everybody, sir."

"Why do they call you that?"

"It's my name, sir."

"What's your father's name?"

"I ain't got none, sir."

"But you know what his name was?"

"No, sir."

"How did you get your name then? It must be the same as your father's, you know."

"Then I suppose my father was Christmas-day, sir, for I know of none else. They always calls me Little Christmas."

"H'm! A little sister of mine, I see," said Uncle Peter to himself.

"Well, who's your mother?"

"My aunt, sir. She knows I'm out, sir."

There was not the least impudence in the child's tone or manner in saying this. She looked up at him with her gipsy eye in the most confident manner. She had not struck him in the least as beautiful; but the longer he looked at her, the more he was pleased with her.

"Is your aunt kind to you?"

"She gives me my wittles."

"Suppose you did not get any money all day, what would she say to you?"

"Oh, she won't give me a hidin' to-day, sir, supposin' I gets no more. You've giv' me enough already, sir; thank you, sir. I'll change it into ha'pence."

"She does beat you sometimes, then?"

"Oh, my!"

Here she rubbed her arms and elbows as if she ached all over at the thought, and these were the only parts she could reach to rub for the whole.

"I *will*," said Uncle Peter to himself.

"Do you think you were born on Christmas-day, little one?"

"I think I was once, sir."

"I shall teach the child to tell lies if I go on asking her questions in this way," thought my uncle. "Will you go home with me?" he said coaxingly.

"Yes, sir, if you will tell me where to put my broom, for I must not go home without it, else aunt would wollop me."

"I will buy you a new broom."

"But aunt would wollop me all the same if I did not bring home the old one for our Christmas fire."

"Never mind. I will take care of you. You may bring your broom if you like, though," he added, seeing a cloud come over the little face.

"Thank you, sir," said the child; and, shouldering her broom, she trotted along behind him, as he led the way home.

But this would not do, either. Before they had gone twelve paces, he had the child in one hand; and before they had gone a second twelve, he had the broom in the other. And so Uncle Peter walked home with his child and his broom. The latter he set down inside the door, and the former he led up to his room. There he seated her on a chair by the fire, and ringing the bell, asked the landlady to bring a basin of bread and milk. The woman cast a look of indignation and wrath at the poor little immortal. She might have been the impersonation of Christmas-day in the catacombs, as she sat with her feet wide apart, and reaching halfway down the legs of the chair, and her black eyes staring from the midst of knotted tangles of hair that never felt comb or brush, or were defended from the wind by bonnet or hood. I dare say my uncle's poor apartment, with its cases of stuffed birds and its square piano that was used for a cupboard, seemed to her the most sumptuous of conceivable abodes. But she said nothing—only stared. When her bread and milk came, she ate it up without a word, and when she had finished it, sat still a moment, as if pondering what it became her to do next. Then she rose, dropped a courtesy, and said:—"Thank you, sir. Please, sir, where's my broom?"

"Oh, but I want you to stop with me, and be my little girl."

"Please, sir, I would rather go to my crossing."

"The face of Little Christmas lengthened visibly, and she was on the point of crying. Uncle Peter saw that he had been too precipitate, and that he must woo the child before he could hope to win her; so he asked her for her address. But though she knew the way to her home perfectly, she could give only what seemed to him the most confused directions how to find it. No doubt to her they seemed as clear as day. Afraid of terrifying her by following her, the best way seemed to him to promise her a new frock on the morrow, if she would come and fetch it. Her face brightened so at the sound of a new frock, that my uncle had very little fear of the fault being hers if she did not come.

"Will you know the way back, my dear?"

"I always know my way anywheres," answered she. So she was allowed to depart with her cherished broom.

Uncle Peter took my mother into council upon the affair of the frock. She thought an old one of my sister's would do best. But my uncle had said a *new* frock, and a new one it must be. So the next day my mother went with him to buy one, and was excessively amused with his entire ignorance of what was suitable for the child. However, the frock being purchased, he saw how absurd it would be to put a new frock over such garments as she must have below, and accordingly made my mother buy everything to clothe her completely. With these treasures he hastened home, and found poor Little Christmas and her broom waiting for him outside the door, for the landlady would not let her in. This roused the wrath of my uncle to such a degree, that, although he had borne wrongs innumerable and aggravated for a long period of years without complaint, he walked in and gave her notice that he would leave in a week. I think she expected he would forget all about it before the day arrived; but with his further designs for Little Christmas, he was not likely to forget it; and I fear I have seldom enjoyed anything so much as the consternation of the woman (whom I heartily hated) when she saw a truck arrive to remove my uncle's few personal possessions from her inhospitable roof. I believe she took her revenge by giving her cronies to understand that she had turned my uncle away at a week's warning for bringing home improper companions to her respectable house.—But to return to Little Christmas. She fared all the better for the landlady's unkindness; for my mother took her home and washed her with her own soft hands from head to foot; and then put all the new clothes on her, and she looked charming. How my uncle would have managed I can't think. He was delighted at the improvement in her appearance. I saw him turn round and wipe his eye with his handkerchief.

"Now, Little Christmas, will you come and live with me?" said he.

She pulled the same face, though not quite so long as before, and said, "I would rather go to my crossing, please, sir."

My uncle heaved a sigh and let her go.

She shouldered her broom as if it had been the rifle of a giant, and trotted away to her work.

But next day, and the next, and the next, she was not to be seen at her wonted corner. When a whole week had passed and she did not make her appearance, my uncle was in despair.

"You see, Charlie," said he, "I am fated to be of no use to anybody, though I was born on Christmas-day."

The very next day, however, being Sunday, my uncle found her as he went to church. She was sweeping a new crossing. She seemed to have found a lower deep still, for, alas! all her new clothes were gone, and she was more tattered and wretched-looking than before. As soon as she saw my uncle she burst into tears.

"Look," she said, pulling up her little frock, and showing her thigh with a terrible bruise on it; "*she* did it."

A fresh burst of tears followed.

"Where are your new clothes, Little Christmas?" asked my uncle.

"She sold them for gin, and then beat me awful. Please, sir, I couldn't help it."

The child's tears were so bitter, that my uncle, without thinking, said—

"Never mind, dear; you shall have another frock."

Her tears ceased, and her face brightened for a moment; but the weeping returned almost instantaneously with increased violence, and she sobbed out:

"It's no use sir; she'd only serve me the same, sir."

"Will you come live with me, then?"

"Yes, please."

She flung her broom from her into the middle of the street, nearly throwing down a cab-horse, betwixt whose fore-legs it tried to pass; then, heedless of the oaths of the man, whom my uncle pacified with a shilling, put her hand in that of her friend and trotted home with him. From that till the day of her death she never left him—of her own accord, at least.

My uncle had, by this time, got into lodgings with a woman of the right sort, who received the little stray lamb with open arms and open heart. Once more she was washed and clothed from head to foot, and from skin to frock. My uncle never allowed her to go out without him, or some one who was capable of protecting her. He did not think it at all necessary to supply the woman, who might not be her aunt after all, with gin unlimited, for the privilege of rescuing Little Christmas from her cruelty. So he felt that she was in great danger of being carried off, for the sake either of her earnings or her ransom; and, in fact, some very suspicious-looking characters were several times observed prowling about the neighbourhood. Uncle Peter, however, took what care he could to prevent any report of this reaching the ears of Little Christmas, lest she should live in terror; and contented himself with watching her carefully. It was some time before our mother would consent to us playing with her freely and beyond her sight; for it was strange to hear the ugly words which would now and then break from her dear little innocent lips. But she was very easily cured of this, although, of course, some time must pass before she could be quite depended upon. She was a sweet-tempered, loving child. But the love seemed for some time to have no way of showing itself, so little had she been used to ways of love and tenderness. When we kissed her she never returned the kiss, but only stared; yet whatever we asked her to do she would do as if her whole heart was in it; and I did not doubt it was. Now I know it was.

After a few years, when Christmas began to be considered tolerably capable of taking care of herself, the vigilance of my uncle gradually relaxed a little. A month before her thirteenth birthday, as near as my uncle could guess, the girl disappeared. She had gone to the day-school as usual, and was expected home in the afternoon; for my uncle would never part with her to go to a boarding-school, and yet wished her to have the benefit of mingling with her fellows, and not being always tied to the button-hole of an old bachelor. But she did not return at the usual hour. My uncle was in despair. He roamed the streets all night; spoke about his child to every policeman he met; went to the station-house of the district, and described her; had bills printed, and offered a hundred pounds reward for her restoration. All was unavailing. The miscreants must have seen the bills, but feared to repose confidence in the offer. Poor Uncle Peter drooped and grew thin. Before the month was out his clothes were hanging about him like a sack. He could hardly swallow a mouthful; hardly even sit down to a meal. I believe he loved his Little Christmas every whit as much as if she had been his own daughter—perhaps more—for he could not help thinking of what she might have been if he had not rescued her; and he felt that God had given her to him as certainly as if she had been his own child, only that she had come in another way. He would get out of bed in the middle of the night, unable to sleep, and go wandering up and down the streets, and into dreadful places, sometimes, to try to find her. But fasting and watching could not go on long without bringing friends with them. Uncle Peter was seized with a fever, which grew and grew till his life was despaired of. He was delirious at times, and then the strangest fancies had possession of his brain. Sometimes he seemed to see the horrid woman she called her aunt, torturing the poor child; sometimes it was old Pagan Father Christmas, clothed in snow and ice, come to fetch his daughter; sometimes it was his old landlady shutting her out in the frost; or himself finding her afterwards, but frozen so hard to the ground that he could not move her to get her indoors. The doctors seemed doubtful, and gave as their opinion—a decided shake of the head.

Christmas-day arrived. In the afternoon, to the wonder of all about him, although he had been wandering a moment before, he suddenly said—

"I was born on Christmas-day, you know. This is the first Christmas-day that didn't bring me good luck."

Turning to me, he added—

"Charlie, my boy, it's a good thing ANOTHER besides me was born on Christmas-day, isn't it?"

"Yes, dear uncle," said I; and it was all I could say. He lay quite quiet for a few minutes, when there came a gentle knock to the street door.

"That's Chrissy!" he cried, starting up in bed, and stretching out his arms with trembling eagerness. "And me to say this Christmas-day would bring no good!"

He fell back on his pillow, and burst into a flood of tears.

I rushed down to the door, and reached it before the servant. I stared. There stood a girl about the size of Chrissy, with an old battered bonnet on, and a ragged shawl. She was standing on the door-step, trembling. I felt she was trembling somehow, for I don't think I saw it. She had Chrissy's eyes too, I thought; but the light was dim now, for the evening was coming on.

All this passed through my mind in a moment, during which she stood silent.

"What is it?" I said, in a tremor of expectation.

"Charlie, don't you know me?" she said, and burst into tears.

We were in each other's arms in a moment—for the first time. But Chrissy is my wife now. I led her up stairs in triumph, and into my uncle's room.

"I knew it was my lamb!" he cried, stretching out his arms, and trying to lift himself up, only he was too weak.

Chrissy flew to his arms. She was very dirty, and her clothes had such a smell of poverty! But there she lay in my uncle's bosom, both of them sobbing, for a long time; and when at last she withdrew, she tumbled down on the floor, and there she lay motionless. I was in a dreadful fright, but my mother came in at the moment, while I was trying to put some brandy within her cold lips, and got her into a warm bath, and put her to bed.

In the morning she was much better, though the doctor would not let her get up for a day or two. I think, however, that was partly for my uncle's sake.

When at length she entered the room one morning, dressed in her old nice clothes, for there were plenty in the wardrobe of her room, my uncle stretched out his arms to her once more, and said:

"Ah! Chrissy, I thought I was going to have my own way, and die on Christmas-day, but it would have been too soon, before I had found you, my darling."

It was resolved that on the same evening, Chrissy should tell my uncle her story. We went out for a walk together; and though she was not afraid to go, the least thing startled her. A voice behind her would make her turn pale and look hurriedly round. Then she would smile again, even before the colour had had time to come back to her cheeks, and say—"What a goose I am! but it is no wonder." I could see too that she looked down at her nice clothes now and then with satisfaction. She does not like me to say so, but she does not deny it either, for Chrissy can't tell a story even about her own feelings. My uncle had given us five pounds each to spend, and that was jolly. We bought each other such a lot of things, besides some for other people. And then we came home and had dinner *tete-a-tete* in my uncle's dining-room; after which we went up to my uncle's room, and sat over the fire in the twilight till his afternoon-nap was over, and he was ready for his tea. This was ready for him by the time he awoke. Chrissy got up on the bed beside him; I got up at the foot of the bed, facing her, and we had the tea-tray and plenty of *etceteras* between us.

"Oh! I *am* happy!" said Chrissy, and began to cry.

"So am I, my darling!" rejoined Uncle Peter, and followed her example.

"So am I," said I, "but I don't mean to cry about it." And then I did.

We all had one cup of tea, and some bread and butter in silence after this. But when Chrissy had poured out the second cup for Uncle Peter, she began of her own accord to tell us her story.

"It was very foggy when we came out of school that afternoon, as you may remember, dear uncle."

"Indeed I do," answered Uncle Peter with a sigh.

"I was coming along the way with Bessie—you know Bessie, uncle—and we stopped to look at a bookseller's window where the gas was lighted. It was full of Christmas things already. One of them I thought very pretty, and I was standing staring at it, when all at once I saw a big drabby woman had poked herself in between Bessie and me. She was staring in at the window too. She was so nasty that I moved away a little from her, but I wanted to have one more look at the picture. The woman came close to me. I moved again. Again she pushed up to me. I looked in her face, for I was rather cross by this time. A horrid feeling, I cannot tell you what it was like, came over me as soon as I saw her. I know how it was now, but I did not know then why I was frightened. I think she saw I was frightened; for she instantly walked against me, and shoved and hustled me round the corner—it was a corner-shop—and before I knew, I was in another street. It was dark and narrow. Just at the moment a man came from the opposite side and joined the woman. Then they caught hold of my hands, and before my fright would let me speak, I was deep into the narrow lane, for they ran with me as fast as they could. Then I began to scream, but they said such horrid words that I was forced to hold my tongue; and in a minute more they had me inside a dreadful house, where the plaster was dropping away from the walls, and the skeleton-ribs of the house were looking through. I was nearly dead with terror and disgust. I don't think it was a bit less dreadful to me from having dim recollections of having known such places well enough at one time of my life. I think that only made me the more frightened, because so the place seemed to have a claim upon me. What if I ought to be there after all, and these dreadful creatures were my father and mother!

"I thought they were going to beat me at once, when the woman, whom I suspected to be my aunt, began to take off my frock. I was dreadfully frightened, but I could not cry. However it was only my clothes that they wanted. But I cannot tell you how frightful it was. They took almost everything I had on, and it was only when I began to scream in despair—sit still, Charlie, it's all over now—that they stopped, with a nod to each other, as much as to say—'we can get the rest afterwards.' Then they put a filthy frock on me; brought me some dry bread to eat; locked the door, and left me. It was nearly dark now. There was no fire. And all my warm clothes were gone.—Do sit still, Charlie.—I was dreadfully cold. There was a wretched-looking bed in one corner, but I think I would have died of cold rather than get into it. And the air in the place was frightful. How long I sat there in the dark, I don't know."

"What did you do all the time?" said I.

"There was only one thing to be done, Charlie. I think that is a foolish question to ask."

"Well, what *did* you do, Chrissy?

"Said my prayers, Charlie."

"And then?"

"Said them again."

"And nothing else?"

"Yes; I tried to get out of the window, but that was of no use; for I could not open it. And it was one story high at least."

"And what did you do next?"

"Said over all my hymns."

"And then—what *did* you do next?"

"Why do you ask me so many times?"

"Because I want to know."

"Well, I will tell you.—I left my prayers alone; and I began at the beginning, and I told God the whole story, as if He had known nothing about it, from the very beginning when Uncle Peter found me on the crossing, down to the minute when I was talking to Him in the dark."

"Ah! my dear," said my uncle, with faltering voice, "you felt better after that, I daresay. And here was I in despair about you, and thought He did not care for any of us. I was very naughty, indeed."

"And what next?" I said.

"By and by I heard a noise of quarrelling in the street, which came nearer and nearer. The door was burst open by some one falling against it. Blundering steps came up the stairs. The two who had robbed me, evidently tipsy, were trying to unlock the door. At length they succeeded, and tumbled into the room."

"'Where is the unnatural wretch,' said the woman, 'who ran away and left her own mother in poverty and sickness?'—

"Oh! uncle, can it be that she is my mother?" said Chrissy, interrupting herself.

"I don't think she is," answered Uncle Peter. "She only wanted to vex you, my lamb. But it doesn't matter whether she is or not."

"Doesn't it, uncle?—I am ashamed of her."

"But you are God's child. And he can't be ashamed of you. For He gave you the mother you had, whoever she was, and never asked you which you would have. So you need not mind. We ought always to like best to be just what God has made us."

"I am sure of that, uncle.—Well, she began groping about to find me, for it was very dark. I sat quite still, except for trembling all over, till I felt her hands on me, when I jumped up, and she fell to the floor. She began swearing dreadfully, but did not try to get up. I crept away to another corner. I heard the man snoring, and the woman breathing loud. Then I felt my way to the door, but, to my horror, found the man lying across it on the floor, so I could not open it. Then I believe I cried for the first time. I was nearly frozen to death, and there was all the long night to bear yet. How I got through it, I cannot tell. It did go away. Perhaps God destroyed some of it for me. But when the light began to come through the window, and show me all the filth of the place, the man and the woman lying on the floor, the woman with her head cut and covered with blood, I began to feel that the darkness had been my friend. I felt this yet more when I saw the state of my own dress, which I had forgotten in the dark. I felt as if I had done some shameful thing, and wanted to follow the darkness, and hide in the skirts of it. It was an old gown of some woollen stuff, but it was impossible to tell what, it was so dirty and worn. I was ashamed that even those drunken creatures should wake and see me in it. But the light would come, and it came and came, until at last it waked them up, and the first words were so dreadful! They quarrelled and swore at each other and at me, until I almost thought there couldn't be a God who would let that go on so, and never stop it. But I suppose He wants them to stop, and doesn't care to stop it Himself, for He could easily do that of course, if He liked."

"Just right, my darling!" said Uncle Peter with emotion.

Chrissy saw that my uncle was too excited by her story although he tried not to show it, and with a wisdom which I have since learned to appreciate, cut it short.

"They did not treat me cruelly, though, the worst was, that they gave me next to nothing to eat. Perhaps they wanted to make me thin and wretched looking, and I believe they succeeded.—Charlie, you'll turn over the cream, if you don't sit still.—Three days passed this way. I have thought all over it, and I think they were a little puzzled how to get rid of me. They had no doubt watched me for a long time, and now they had got my clothes, they were afraid.—At last one night they took me out. My aunt, if aunt she is, was respectably dressed—that is, comparatively, and the man had a great-coat on, which covered his dirty clothes. They helped me into a cart which stood at the door, and drove off. I resolved to watch the way we went. But we took so many turnings through narrow streets before we came out in a main road, that I soon found it was all one mass of confusion in my head; and it was too dark to read any of the names of the streets, for the man kept as much in the middle of the road as possible. We drove some miles, I should think, before we stopped at the gate of a small house, where an elderly lady stood, holding the door half open. When we reached it, my aunt gave me a sort of shove in, saying to the lady, 'There she is.' Then she said to me: 'Come now be a good girl and don't tell lies,' and turning hastily, ran down the steps, and got into the cart at the gate, which drove off at once the way we had come. The lady looked at me from head to foot sternly but kindly too, I thought, and so glad was I to find myself clear of those dreadful creatures, that I burst out crying. She instantly began to read a lecture on the privilege of being placed with Christian people, who would instruct me how my soul might be saved, and teach me to lead an honest and virtuous life. But as often as I opened my mouth to tell anything about myself or my uncle, or, indeed, to say anything at all, I was stopped by her saying—'Now don't tell lies. Whatever you do, don't tell lies.' This shut me up quite. I could not speak when I knew she would not believe me. But I did not cry, I only felt my face get very hot, and somehow my back-bone grew longer, though I felt my eyes fixed on the ground.

"'But,' she went on, 'you must change your dress. I will show you the way to your room, and you will find a print gown there, which I hope you will keep clean. And above all things don't tell lies.'

Here Chrissy burst out laughing, as if it was such fun to be accused of lying; but presently her eyes filled, and she made haste to go on.

"You may be sure I made haste to put on the nice clean frock, and, to my delight, found other clean things for me as well. I declare I felt like a princess for a whole day after, notwithstanding the occupation. For I soon found that I had been made over to Mrs. Sphinx, as a servant of all work. I think she must have paid these people for the chance of reclaiming one whom they had represented as at least a great liar. Whether my wages were to be paid to them, or even what they were to be, I never heard. I made up my mind at once that the best thing would be to do the work without grumbling, and do it as well as I could, for that would be doing no harm to anyone, but the contrary, while it would give me the better chance of making my escape. But though I was determined to get away the first opportunity, and was miserable when I thought how anxious you would all be about me, yet I confess it was such a relief to be clean and in respectable company, that I caught myself singing once or twice the very first day. But the old lady soon stopped that. She was about in the kitchen the greater part of the day till almost dinner-time, and taught me how to cook and save my soul both at once."

"Indeed," interrupted Uncle Peter, "I have read receipts for the salvation of the soul that sounded very much as if they came out of a cookery-book." And the wrinkles of his laugh went up into his night-cap, Neither Chrissy nor I understood this at the time, but I have often thought of it since.

Chrissy went on:

"I had finished washing up my dinner-things, and sat down for a few minutes, for I was tired. I was staring into the fire, and thinking and thinking how I should get away, and what I should do when I got out of the house, and feeling as if the man and the woman were always prowling about it, and watching me through the window, when suddenly I saw a little boy in a corner of the kitchen, staring at me with great brown eyes. He was a little boy, perhaps about six years old, with a pale face, and very earnest look. I did not speak to him, but waited to see what he would do. A few minutes passed, and I forgot him. But as I was wiping my eyes, which would get wet sometimes, notwithstanding my good-fortune, he came up to me, and said in a timid whisper,

"'Are you a princess?'

"'What makes you think that?' I said.

"'You have got such white hands,' he answered.

"'No, I am not a princess,' I said.

"'Aren't you Cinderella?'

"'No, my darling,' I replied; 'but something like her; for they have stolen me away from my home and brought me here. I wish I could get away.'

"And here I confess I burst into a down right fit of crying.

"'Don't cry,' said the little fellow, stroking my cheek. 'I will let you out some time. Shall you be able to find your way home all by yourself?'

"'Yes I think so,' I answered; but at the same time, I felt very doubtfil about it, because I always fancied those people watching me. But before either of us spoke again, in came Mrs. Sphinx.

"'You naughty boy! What business have you to make the servant neglect her work?'

"For I was still sitting by the fire, and my arm was round the dear little fellow, and his head was leaning on my shoulder.

"'She's not a servant, auntie!' cried he, indignantly. 'She's a real princess, though of course she won't own to it.'

"'What lies you have been telling the boy! You ought to be ashamed of yourself. Come along directly. Get the tea at once, Jane.'

"My little friend went with his aunt, and I rose and got the tea. But I felt much lighter-hearted since I had the sympathy of the little boy to comfort me. Only I was afraid they would make him hate me. But, although I saw very little of him the rest of the time, I knew they had not succeeded in doing so; for as often as he could, he would come sliding up to me, saying 'How do you do, princess?' and then run away, afraid of being seen and scolded.

"I was getting very desperate about making my escape, for there was a high wall about the place, and the gate was always locked at night. When Christmas-eve came, I was nearly crazy with thinking that tomorrow was uncle's birthday; and that I should not be with him. But that very night, after I had gone to my room, the door opened, and in came little Eddie in his nightgown, his eyes looking very bright and black over it.

"'There, princess! said he, there is the key of the gate. Run.'

"I took him in my arms and kissed him, unable to speak. He struggled to get free, and ran to the door. There he turned and said:

"'You will come back and see me some day—will you not?'

"'That I will,' I answered.

"'That you shall,' said Uncle Peter.

"I hid the key, and went to bed, where I lay trembling. As soon as I was sure they must be asleep, I rose and dressed. I had no bonnet or shawl but those I had come in; and though they disgusted me, I thought it better to put them on. But I dared not unlock the street-door for fear of making a noise. So I crept out of the kitchen-window, and then I got out at the gate all safe. No one was in sight. So I locked it again, and threw the key over. But what a time of fear and wandering about I had in the darkness, before I dared to ask any one the way. It was a bright, clear night; and I walked very quietly till I came upon a great wide common. The sky, and the stars, and the wideness frightened me, and made me gasp at first. I felt as if I should fall away from everything into nothing. And it was so lonely! But then I thought of God, and in a moment I knew that what I had thought loneliness was really the presence of God. And then I grew brave again, and walked on. When the morning dawned, I met a bricklayer going to his work; and found that I had been wandering away from London all the time; but I did not mind that. Now I turned my face towards it, though not the way I had come. But I soon got dreadfully tired and faint, and once I think I fainted quite. I went up to a house, and asked for a piece of bread, and they gave it to me, and I felt much better after eating it. But I had to rest so often, and got so tired, and my feet got so sore, that—you know how late it was before I got home to my darling uncle."

"And me too!" I expostulated.

"And you, too, Charlie," she answered; and we all cried over again.

"This shan't happen any more!" said my uncle.

After tea was over, he asked for writing things, and wrote a note, which he sent off.

The next morning, about eleven, as I was looking out of the window, I saw a carriage drive up and stop at the door.

"What a pretty little brougham!" I cried. "And such a jolly horse! Look here, Chrissy!"

Presently Uncle Peter's bell rang, and Miss Chrissy was sent for. She came down radiant with pleasure.

"What do you think, Charlie! That carriage is mine—all my own. And I am to go to school in it always. Do come and have a ride in it."

You may be sure I was delighted to do so.

"Where shall we go?" I said.

"Let us ask uncle if we may go and see the little darling who set me free."

His consent was soon obtained, and away we went. It was a long drive, but we enjoyed it beyond everything. When we reached the house, we were shown into the drawing-room.

There was Mrs. Sphinx and little Eddie. The lady stared; but the child knew Cinderella at once, and flew into her arms.

"I knew you were a princess!" he cried. "There, auntie!"

But Mrs. Sphinx had put on an injured look, and her hands shook very much.

"Really, Miss Belper, if that is your name, you have behaved in a most unaccountable way. Why did you not tell me, instead of stealing the key of the gate, and breaking the kitchen window? A most improper way for a young lady to behave—to run out of the house at midnight!"

"You forget, madam," replied Chrissy, with more dignity than I had ever seen her assume, "that as soon as ever I attempted to open my mouth, you told me not to tell lies. You believed the wicked people who brought me here rather than myself. However, as you will not be friendly, I think we had better go. Come, Charlie?"

"Don't go, princess," pleaded little Eddie.

"But I must, for your auntie does not like me," said Chrissy.

"I am sure I always meant to do my duty by you. And I will do so still.—Beware, my dear young woman, of the deceitfulness of riches. Your carriage won't save your soul!"

Chrissy was on the point of saying something rude, as she confessed when we got out; but she did not. She made her bow, turned and walked away. I followed, and poor Eddie would have done so too, but was laid hold of by his aunt. I confess this was not quite proper behaviour on Chrissy's part; but I never discovered that till she made me see it. She was very sorry afterwards, and my uncle feared the brougham had begun to hurt her already, as she told me. For she had narrated the whole story to him, and his look first let her see that she had been wrong. My uncle went with her afterwards to see Mrs. Sphinx, and thank her for having done her best; and to take Eddie such presents as my uncle only knew how to buy for children. When he went to school, I know he sent him a gold watch. From that time till now that she is my wife, Chrissy has had no more such adventures; and if Uncle Peter did not die on Christmas-day, it did not matter much, for Christmas-day makes all the days of the year as sacred as itself.

An Old Scot's Christmas Story
(Papa's Story)

"O tell us a story, papa," said a wise-faced little girl, one winter night, as she intermitted for a moment her usual occupation of the hour before bedtime—that, namely, of sucking her thumb, earnestly and studiously followed, as if the fate of the world lay on the faithfulness of the process; "Do tell us a story, papa."

"Yes, do, papa," chimed in several more children. It is *such* a long time since you told us a story."

"I don't think papa ever told us a story," said one of the youngest.

"Oh, Dolly!" exclaimed half a dozen. But her next elder sister took up the speech.

"Yes, I dare say. But you were only born last year, and papa has been away for months and months."

Now, Dolly was five, and her papa had been away for three weeks.

"Well," interposed their papa, "I will try. What shall it be about?"

"Oh! about Scotland," cried the eldest.

"Why do you want a story about Scotland?"

"Because you will like it best yourself, papa."

"I don't want one about Scotland. I'm not a Scotchman, though papa is," cried Dolly, "I'm an Englishman."

"I like Scotch stories," said the sucker of thumbs; "only I can't understand the curious words. They sound so rough, I never can understand them."

"Well, my darlings, I will tell you one about Scotland, and there shan't be a Scotch word in it. If one single one comes out of my mouth you may punish me anyway you please."

"Oh, that's jolly! How shall we punish papa if he says one Scotch word?"

"Pull his beard!" said Dolly.

"No, that would be rude!" cried three or four.

Whereupon Dolly's face changed, and she took to her thumb, like Katy.

"Make him pay a fine."

"That's no use, papa's so rich!"

Whereas the chief difficulty papa had in telling a story was the thought of the butcher's bill popping in through twenty different keyholes.

"Make him pay a kiss to each of us for every word!"

"No, that would stop the story!"

"Kiss him to death when it's done!"

"Yes!—yes!—yes—kiss him to death when it's done!"

So it was agreed; and papa began."

"You know, my darlings, there are a great many hills in Scotland, which are green with grass to the very top, and the sheep feed all over them?"

"Oh, yes! I know! Like Hampstead-hill."

"No. Like that place in the City—Ludgate-hill."

"No, my dears; not like either of those. Just come to the window, and I will try to show you. You see that star shining so brightly away there?"

"Yes, but that is not a hill, papa; it's a star!"

"Yes, it's a star. But suppose you could not see that star for a great heap of rock and earth and stone rising up between you and the star, covered with grass, and with streams running down its sides in every direction, that heap would be a hill. And in some parts of Scotland there are a great many of these hills crowded together, only divided from each other by deep places called valleys. They all grow out of one root—that is the earth. The tops of these hills are high up and lonely in the air, with the stars above them, and often the clouds round about them like torn garments."

"What's *garments*, Kitty?"

"Frocks, Dolly."

"What tears them, then?"

"The wind tears them; and goes roaring and raving about the hills; and makes such a noise against the steep rocks, running into the holes in them and out again, that those hills are sometimes very awful places. But in the sunshine, although they do look lonely, they are so bright and beautiful, that the boys and girls fancy the way to heaven lies up those hills."

"And doesn't it?"

"No."

"Where is it, then?"

"Ah! that's just what you come here to find out. But you must let me go on with my story now. In the winter, on the other hand, they are such wild howling places, with the hard hailstones beating upon them, and the soft, smothering snowflakes heaping up dreadful wastes of whiteness upon them, that if ever there was a child out on them he would die with fear, if he did not die with cold. But there are only sheep there, and they don't stay very high up the hills when the winter once begins to come over the mountains."

"What's mountains?"

"Mountains are higher hills yet."

"Higher yet! They can't be higher yet."

"Oh! yes, they are; and there are higher and higher yet, till you could hardly believe it, even when you saw them.

"Well, as the winter comes over the tops of the hills the sheep come down their sides, because it is warmer the lower down you come; and even a foot thick of wool on their backs and sides could not keep up the terrible cold up there.

"But the sheep are not very knowing creatures, so they are something better instead. They are wise—that is, they are obedient—creatures, obedience being the very best wisdom. For, because they are not very knowing, they have a man to take care of them, who knows where to take them, especially when a storm comes on. Not that the sheep are so very silly as not to know where to go to get out of the wind, but they don't and can't think that some ways of getting out of danger are more dangerous still. They would lie down in a quiet place, and lie there till the snow settled down over them and smothered them. They would not feel it cold, their wool is so thick. Or they would tumble down steep places and be killed, or buried in the snow, or carried away by the stream at the bottom. So, though they know a little, they don't know enough, and need a shepherd to take care of them.

"Now the shepherd, though he is wise, is not quite clever enough for all that is wanted of him up in those strange, terrible hills; and he needs another to help him. Now, who do you think helps the shepherd? Ah! you know, Maggy; but you mustn't tell. I will tell. It is a curious creature with four legs—the shepherd has only two, you know;—and he is covered all over with long hair of three different colours mixed—black, and brown, and white; and he has a long nose and a longer tongue, which he knows how to hold. This tongue it is a great comfort to him sometimes to hang out of his mouth as far as ever it will hang. And he has still a longer tail, which is a greater comfort to him yet. I don't know what ever he would do without his tail; for, when his master speaks kindly to him, he is so full of delight, that I think he would die if he hadn't his tail to wag. He lets his gladness off by wagging his tail, so that it shan't burst his dear, honest, good dog-heart. Ah! there, I've told you. He's a dog, you see; and the very wisest and cleverest of all dogs. He could be taught anything. Only he is such a gentleman, though dressed very plainly, as a great many gentlemen are, that it would be a shame to teach him some of the things they teach commonplace rich dogs.

"Well, the shepherd tells the dog what he wants done, and off the dog runs to do it; for he can run three times as fast as the shepherd, and can get up and down places much better. I am not sure that he can see better than the shepherd, but I know he can smell better. So that he is just four legs and a long nose to the shepherd, besides the love he gives him which would comfort any good man, even if it were offered him by a hedgehog or a hen. And for this understanding, if I were to tell Willie how much I believe he understands—if I weren't his papa, that is—Willie, there, who has such a high opinion of his own judgment, and shakes his head so knowingly when he hears anything for the first time, as if were a shame for anything to come into existence without letting him know first—Willie, I say, would consider me silly for believing it, or, what would be a great deal worse, would think that I didn't really believe it, though I said it.

"One evening, in the beginning of April, the weakly sun of the season had gone down with a pale face behind the shoulder of a hill in the background of my story. If you had been there and had climbed up that hill, you would have seen him a great while longer, provided he had not, in the mean time, set behind a mountain of cloud, which, at this season of the year, he was very ready to do, and which, I suspect, he actually did this very evening about which I am telling you. And because he has gone down the peat-fires upon the hearths of the cottages all began to glow more brightly, as if they were glad he was gone at last and had left them their work to do—or, rather, as if they wanted to do all they could to make up for his absence. And on one hearth in particular the peat-fire glowed very brightly. There was a pot hanging over it, with supper in it; and there was a little girl sitting by it, with a sweet, thoughtful face. Her hair was done up in a silken net, for it was the custom with Scotch girls—they wore no bonnet—to have their hair so arranged, many years before it became a fashion in London. She had a bunch of feathers, not in her hair, but fastened to her side by her apron-string, in the quill-ends of which was stuck the end of one of her knitting-needles, while the other was loose in her hand. But both were fast and busy in the loops of a blue-ribbed stocking, which she was knitting for her father.

"He was out on the hills. He had that morning taken his sheep higher up than before, and Nelly knew this; but it could not be long now till she would hear his footsteps, and measure the long stride between which brought him and happiness together."

"But hadn't she a mother?"

"Oh! yes, she had. If you had been in the cottage that night you would have heard a cough every now and then, and would have found that Nelly's mother was lying in a bed in the room—not a bed with curtains, but a bed with doors like a press. This does not seem a nice way of having a bed; but we should all be glad of the wooden curtain about us at night if we lived in such a cottage, on the side of a hill along which the wind swept like a wild river, only ten times faster than any river would run even down the hillside. Through the cottage it would be spouting, and streaming, and eddying, and fighting, all night long, and a poor woman with a cough, or a man who has been out in the cold all day, is very glad of such a place to lie in, and leave the rest of the house to the wind and the fairies.

"Nelly's mother was ill, and there was little hope of her getting well again. What she could have done without Nelly, I can't think. It was so much easier to be ill with Nelly sitting there. For she was a good Nelly.

After a while Nelly rose and put some peats on the fire, and hung the pot a link or two higher on the chain; for she was a wise creature, though she was only twelve, and could cook very well, because she took trouble, and thought about it. Then she sat down to her knitting again, which was a very frugal amusement.

"'I wonder what's keeping your father, Nelly,' said her mother from the bed.

"'I don't know, mother. It's not been very late yet. He'll be home by and by. You know he was going over the shoulder of the hill to-day.'

"Now that was the same shoulder of the hill that the sun went down behind. And at the moment the sun was going down behind it, Nelly's father was standing on the top of it, and Nelly was looking up to the very place where he stood, and yet she did not see him. He was not too far off to be seen, but the sun was in her eyes, and the light of the sun hid him from her. He was then coming across with the sheep, to leave them for the night in a sheltered place—within a circle of stones that would keep the wind off them, and he ought, by rights, to have been home at least half an hour ago.—At length Nelly heard the distant sound of a heavy shoe upon the point of a great rock that grew up from the depths of the earth and just came through the surface of the path leading across the furze and brake to their cottage. She always watched for that sound—the sound of her father's shoe, studded thick with broad-headed nails, upon the top of that rock. She started up; but instead of rushing out to meet him, went to the fire and lowered the pot.

Then taking up a wooden bowl, half full of oatmeal neatly pressed down into it, with a little salt on the top, she proceeded to make a certain dish for her father's supper, of which strong Scotchmen are very fond. By the time her father reached the door, it was ready, and set down with a plate over it to keep it hot, though it had a great deal more need, I think, to be let cool a little.

"When he entered, he looked troubled. He was a tall man, dressed in rough grey cloth, with a broad, round, blue bonnet, as they call it. His face looked as if it had been weather-beaten into peace."

"Beaten into pieces, papa! How dreadful!"

"Be quiet, Dolly; that's not what papa means."

"I want to know, then."

"Well, Dolly, I think it would take twenty years at least to make it plain to you, so I had better go on with my story, especially as you will come to understand it one day without my explaining it. The shepherd's face, I say, was weather-beaten and quiet, with large, grand features, in which the docility of his dogs and the gentleness of his sheep were mingled with the strength and wisdom of a man who had to care for both dogs and sheep.

"'Well, Nelly,' he said, laying his hand on her forehead as she looked up into his face, 'how's your mother?'

"And without waiting for an answer he went down to the bed, where the pale face of his wife lay upon the pillow. She held out her thin, white hand to him, and he took it up so gently in his strong, brown hand. But, before he had spoken, she saw the trouble on his face, and said,

"'What has made you so late to-night, John?'

"'I was nearly at the fold,' said the shepherd, 'before I saw that one of the lambs was missing. So, after I got them all in, I went back with the dogs to look for him.'

"'Where's Jumper, then?' asked Nelly, who had been patting the neck and stroking the ears of the one dog which had followed the shepherd's heels, and was now lying before the fire, enjoying the warmth none the less that he had braved the cold all day without minding it a bit.

"'When we couldn't see anything of the lamb,' replied her father, 'I told Jumper to go after him and bring him to the house; and Blackfoot and I came home together. I doubt he'll have a job of it, poor dog! for it's going to be a rough night; but if dog can bring him, he will.'

"As the shepherd stopped speaking he seated himself by the fire and drew the wooden bowl towards him. Then he lifted his blue bonnet from his head, and said grace, half aloud, half murmured to himself. Then he put his bonnet on his head again, for his head was rather bald, and, as I told you, the cottage was a draughty place. And just as he put it on, a blast of wind struck the cottage and roared in the wide chimney. The next moment the rain dashed against the little window of four panes, and fell hissing into the peat-fire.

"'There it comes,' said the shepherd.

"'Poor Jumper!' said Nelly.

"'And poor little lamb!' said the shepherd.

"'It's the lamb's own fault,' said Nelly; 'he shouldn't have run away.'

"'Ah! yes,' returned her father; 'but then the lamb didn't know what he was about exactly.'

"When the shepherd had finished his supper, he rose and went out to see whether Jumper and the lamb were coming; but the dark night would have made the blackest dog and the whitest lamb both of one colour, and he soon came in again. Then he took the Bible and read a chapter to his wife and daughter, which did them all good, even though Nelly did not understand very much of it. And then he prayed a prayer, and was very near praying for Jumper and the lamb, only he could not quite. And there he was wrong. He should have prayed about whatever troubled him or could be done good to. But he was such a good man that I am almost ashamed of saying he was wrong.

"And just as he came to the *Amen* in his prayer, there came a whine to the door. And he rose from his knees and went and opened the door. And there was the lamb with Jumper behind him. And Jumper looked dreadfully wet, and draggled, and tired, and the curls had all come out of his long hair. And yet he seemed as happy as a dog could be, and looked up in the face of the shepherd triumphantly, as much as to say, 'Here he is, Master!' And the lamb looked scarcely anything the worse; for his thick, oily wool had kept away the wet; and he hadn't been running about everywhere looking for Jumper as Jumper had been for him.

"And Jumper, after Nelly had given him his supper, lay down by the fire beside the other dog, which made room for him to go next to the glowing peats; and the lamb, which had been eating all day and didn't want any supper, lay down beside him. And then Nelly bade her father and mother and the dogs good-night, and went away to bed likewise, thinking the wind might blow as it pleased now, for sheep and dogs, and father and all, were safe for the whole of the dark, windy hours between that and the morning. It is so nice to know that there is a long *nothing to do*;—but only after everything is done.

"But there are other winds in the world besides those which shake the fleeces of sheep and the beards of men, or blow ships to the bottom of the sea, or scatter the walls of cottages abroad over the hillsides. There are winds that blow up huge storms inside the hearts of men and women, and blow till the great clouds full of tears go up, and rain down from the eyes to quiet them.

"What can papa mean?"

"Never you mind, Dolly. You'll know soon enough. I'm fourteen and I know what papa means."

"Nelly lay down in her warm bed, feeling as safe and snug as ever child felt in a large, rich house in a great city. For there was the wind howling outside to make it all the quieter inside; and there was the great, bare, cold hill before the window, which, although she could not see it, and only knew that it was there, made the bed in which she lay so close, and woolly, and warm. Now this bed was separated from her father and mother's only by a thin partition, and she heard them talking. And they had not talked long before that other cold wind that was blowing through their hearts blew into hers too. And I will tell you what they said to each other that made the cold wind blow into her heart.

"'It wasn't the loss of the lamb, John, that made you look so troubled when you came home to-night,' said her mother.

"'No, it wasn't, Jane, I must confess,' returned her father.

"'You've heard something about Harry.'

"'I can't deny it.'

"'What is it?'

"'I'll tell you in the morning.'

"'I shan't sleep a wink for thinking whatever it can be, John. You had better tell me now. If the Lord would only bring that stray lamb back to his fold, I should die happy—sorry as I should be to leave Nelly and you, my own John.'

"'Don't talk about dying, Nelly. It breaks my heart.'

"'We won't talk about it, then. But what's this about Harry? And how came you to hear it?'

"'I was close to the hill-road, when I saw James Jamieson, the carrier, coming up the hill with his cart. I ran and met him.'

"'And he told you? What did he tell you?'

"'Nothing very particular. He only hinted that he had heard, from Wauchope the merchant, that a certain honest man's son—he meant me, Nelly—was going the wrong road. And I said to James Jamieson—What road could the man mean? And James said to me—He meant the broad

road, of course. And I sat down on a stone, and I heard no more; at least, I could not make sense of what James went on to say; and when I lifted my head, James and his cart were just out of sight over the top of the hill. I dare say that was how I lost the lamb.'

"A deep silence followed, and Nelly understood that her mother could not speak. At length a sob and a low weeping came through the boards to her keen mountain ear. But not another word was spoken; and, although Nelly's heart was sad, she soon fell fast asleep.

"Now, Willie had gone to college, and had been a very good boy for the first winter. They go to college only in winter in Scotland. And he had come home in the end of March and had helped his father to work their little farm, doing his duty well to the sheep and to everything and to everybody; for learning had not made him the least unfit for work. Indeed, work that learning does really make a man unfit for, cannot be fit for that man—perhaps is not fit work for anybody. When Winter came, he had gone back to Edinburgh, and he ought to have been home a week ago, and he had not come. He had written to say he had to finish some lessons he had begun to give, and could not be home till the end of the month. Now this was so far true that it was not a lie. But there was more in it: he did not want to go home to the lonely hillside—so lonely that there were only a father and a mother and a sister there. He had made acquaintance with some students who were fonder of drinking whisky than of getting up in the morning to write abstracts, and he didn't want to leave them.

"Nelly was, as I have said, too young to keep awake because she was troubled; and so, before half an hour was over, was fast asleep and dreaming. And the wind outside, tearing the thatch of the cottage, mingled with her dream.

"I will tell you what her dream was.—She thought they were out in the dark and the storm, she and her father. But she was no longer Nelly, she was Jumper. And her father said to her, 'Jumper, go after the black lamb and bring him home.' And away she galloped over the stones, and through the furze, and across the streams, and up the rocks, and jumped the stone fences, and swam the pools of water, to find the little black lamb. And all the time, some how or other, the little black lamb was her brother Willie. And nothing could turn the dog Jumper, though the wind blew as if it would blow him off all his four legs, and off the hill, as one blows a fly off a book. And the hail beat in Jumper's face, as if it would put out his eyes or knock holes in his forehead, and yet Jumper went on."

"But it wasn't Jumper; it was Nelly, you know."

"I know that, but I am talking about the dog Jumper, that Nelly thought she was. He went on and on, and over the top of the cold, wet hill, and was beginning to grow hopeless about finding the black lamb, when, just a little way down the other side, he came upon him behind a rock. He was standing in a miry pool, all wet with rain. Jumper would never have found him, the night was so dark and the lamb was so black, but that he gave a bleat; whereupon Jumper tried to say 'Willie', but could not, and only gave a gobbling kind of bark. So he jumped upon the lamb, and taking a mouthful of his wool, gave him a shake that made him pull his feet out of the mire, and then drove him off before him, trotting all the way home. When they came into the cottage, the black lamb ran up to Nelly's mother, and jumped into her bed, and Jumper jumped in after him; and then Nelly was Nelly and Willie was Willie, as they used to be, when Nelly would creep into Willie's bed in the morning and kiss him awake. Then Nelly woke, and was sorry that it was a dream. For Willie was still away, far off on the broad road, and however was he to be got home? Poor black lamb!

"She soon made up her mind. Only how to carry out her mind was the difficulty. All day long she thought about it. And she wrote a letter to her father, telling him what she was going to do; and when she went to her room the next night, she laid the letter on her bed, and, putting on her Sunday bonnet and cloak, waited till they should be asleep.

"The shepherd had gone to sleep very sad. He, too, had been writing a letter. It had taken him all the evening to write, and Nelly had watched his face as he wrote it, and seen how the muscles of it worked with sorrow and pain as he slowly put word after word down on the paper. When he had finished it, and folded it up, and put a wafer on it, and addressed it, he left it on the table, and, as I said, went to bed, where he soon fell asleep; for even sorrow does not often keep people awake that have worked hard through the day in the open air. And Nelly was watching.

"When she thought he was asleep, she took a pair of stockings out of a chest and put them in her pocket. Then, taking her Sunday shoes in her hand, she stepped gently from her room to the cottage door, which she opened easily, for it was never locked. She then found that it was pitch dark; but she could keep the path well enough, for her bare feet told her at once when she was going off it. It is a great blessing to have bare feet. People with bare feet can always keep the path better, and keep their garments cleaner, too. Only they must be careful to wash them at night.

"So, dark as it was, she soon reached the road. There was no wind that night, and the clouds hid the stars. She would turn in the direction of Edinburgh, and let the carrier overtake her. For she felt rather guilty, and was anxious to get on.

"After she had walked a good while, she began to wonder that the carrier had not come up with her. The fact is that the carrier never left till the early morning. She was not a bit afraid, though, reasoning that, as she was walking in the same direction, it would take him so much the longer to get up with her.

"At length, after walking a long way—longer far than she thought, for she walked a great part of it half asleep—she began to feel a little tired, and sat down upon a stone by the roadside. There was a stone behind her, too. She could just see its grey face. She leaned her back against it, and fell asleep.

"When she woke she could not think where she was, or how she got there. It was a dark, drizzly morning, and her feet were cold. But she was quite dry for the rock against which she fell asleep in the night projected so far over her head that it had kept all the rain off her. She could not have chosen a better place, if she had been able to choose. But the night around her was very dreary. In front lay a swampy ground, creeping away, dismal and wretched, to the horizon, where a long low hill closed it. Behind her rose a mountain, bare and rocky, on which neither sheep nor shepherd was to be seen. Her home seemed to have vanished in the night, and left her either in a dream or in another world. And as she came to herself, the fear grew upon her that either she had missed the way in the dark or the carrier had gone past while she slept, either of which was dreadful to contemplate. She began to feel hungry, too, and she had not had the foresight to bring even a piece of oatcake with her.

"It was only dusky dawn yet. There was plenty of time. She would sit down again for a little while; for the rock had a homely look to her. It had been her refuge all night, and she was not willing to leave it. So she leaned her arms on her knees, and gazed out upon the dreary, grey, misty flat before her.

"Then she rose, and turning her back on the waste, kneeled down, and prayed God that, as he taught Jumper to find lambs, he would teach her to find her brother. And thus she fell fast asleep again.

"When she awoke once more and turned towards the road, whom should she see standing there but the carrier, staring at her. And his big strong horses stood in the road too, with their carts behind them. They were not in the least surprised. She could not help crying, just a little, for joy.

"'Why, Nelly, what on earth are you doing here?' said the carrier.

"'Waiting for you,' answered Nelly.

"'Where are you going, child?'

"'To Edinburgh.'

"'What on earth are you going to do in Edinburgh?'

"'I am going to my brother Willie, at the college.'

"'But the college is over now.'

"'I know that,' said Nelly.

"'It's a lucky thing that I know, then. But you have no business to leave home this way.'

"'Oh! yes, I have.'

"'I am sure your father did not know of it, for when he gave me a letter this morning to take to Willie he did not say a word about you.'

"'He thought I was asleep in my bed,' returned Nelly, trying to smile. But the thought that the carrier had actually seen her father since she left home, was too much for her, and she cried.

"'I can't go back with you now,' said the carrier, 'so you must go on with me.'

"'That's just what I want,' said Nelly.

"So the carrier made her put on her shoes and stockings, for he was a kind man and had children of his own. Then he pulled out some of the straw that packed his cart, and made her a little bed on the tarpaulin that covered it, just where there was a soft bundle beneath. Then he lifted her up on it and covered her over with a few empty sacks. There Nelly was so happy, and warm, and comfortable, that, for the third time, she fell asleep.

"When she woke he gave her some bread and cheese for her breakfast, and some water out of a brook that crossed the road, and then Nelly began to look about her. The rain had ceased and the sun was shining, and the country looked very pleasant; but Nelly thought it a strange country. She could see much farther! And corn was growing everywhere, and there was not a sheep to be seen, and there were many cows feeding in the fields.

"'Are we near Edinburgh?' she asked.

"'Oh, no!' answered the carrier; 'we are a long way from Edinburgh yet.'

"And so they journeyed on. The day was flecked all over with sunshine and rain; and when the rain's turn came, Nelly would creep under a corner of the tarpaulin till it was over. They slept part of the night at a small town they passed through.

"Nelly thought it a very long way to Edinburgh, though the carrier was kind to her, and gave her of everything he had himself, except the whisky, which he did not think good for her.

"At length she spied, far away, a great hill, that looked like a couching lion.

"'Do you see that hill?' said the carrier.

"'I am just looking at it,' answered Nelly.

"'Edinburgh lies at the foot of that hill.'

"'Oh!' said Nelly; and scarcely took her eyes off it till it went out of sight again.

"Reaching the brow of an eminence, they saw Arthur's Seat (as the carrier said the hill was called) once more, and below it a great jagged ridge of what Nelly took to be broken rocks. But the carrier told her that was the Old Town of Edinburgh. Those fierce-looking splinters on the edge of the mass were the roofs, gables, and chimneys of the great houses once inhabited by the nobility of Scotland. But when you came near the houses you find them shabby-looking; for they are full of poor people, who cannot keep them clean and nice.

"But, certainly, my children, if you will excuse your Scotch papa for praising his own country's capital, I don't believe there ever was a city that looked so grand from the distance as that Old Town of Edinburgh. And when you get into the streets you can fancy yourself hundreds of years back in the story of Scotland. Seen thus through the perspective of time or distance, it is a great marvel to everyone with any imagination at all; and it was nothing less to little Nelly, even when she got into the middle of it. But her heart was so full of its dog-duties towards her black lamb of a brother that the toyshops and the sugar-plum-shops could not draw it towards their minds of wonder and wealth.

"At length the cart stopped at a public-house in the Grassmarket—a wide, open place, with strange old houses all round it, and a huge rock, with a castle on its top, towering over it. There Nelly got down.

"'I can't go with you till I've unloaded my cart,' said the carrier.

"'I don't want you to go with me, please.' said Nelly. 'I think Willie would rather not. Please give me father's letter.'"

"So the carrier gave her the letter, and got a little boy of the landlady's to show her the way up the West-bow—a street of tall houses, so narrow that you might have shaken hands across it from window to window. But those houses are all pulled down now, I am sorry to say, and the street Nelly went up has vanished. From the West-bow they came up a stair into the High-street, and thence into a narrow court, and then up a winding stair, and so came to the floor where Willie's lodging was. There the little boy left Nelly.

"Nelly knocked two or three times before anybody came; and when at last a woman opened the door, what do you think that woman did the moment she inquired after Willie?—She shut the door in her face with a fierce, scolding word. For Willie had vexed her that morning, and she thoughtlessly took her revenge upon Nelly without even asking her a question. Then, indeed, for a moment, Nelly's courage gave way. All at once she felt dreadfully tired, and sat down upon the stair and cried. And the landlady was so angry with Willie that she forgot all about the little girl who wanted to see him.

"So for a full hour Nelly sat upon the stair, moving only to let people pass. She felt dreadfully miserable, but had no courage to knock again, for fear of having the door shut in her face yet more hopelessly. At last a woman came up and knocked at the door. Nelly rose trembling and stood behind her. The door opened; the woman was welcomed; she entered. The door was again closing when Nelly cried out in agony,

"'Please, ma'am, I want to see my brother Willie!' and burst into sobs.

"The landlady, her wrath having this time assuaged, was vexed with herself and ashamed that she had not let the child in.

"'Bless me!' she cried; 'have you been there all this time? Why didn't you tell me you were Willie's sister? Come in. You won't find him in, though. It's not much of his company we get, I can tell you.'

"'I don't want to come in, then,' sobbed Nelly. 'Please to tell me where he is, ma'am.'

"'How should I know where he is? At no good, I warrant. But you had better come in and wait, for it's your only chance of seeing him before to-morrow morning.'

"With a sore heart Nelly went in and sat down by the kitchen fire. And the landlady and her visitor sat and talked together, every now and then casting a look at Nelly, who kept her eyes on the ground, waiting with all her soul till Willie should come. Every time the landlady looked, she looked sooner the next time; and every time she looked, Nelly's sad face went deeper into her heart; so that, before she knew what was going on herself, she quite loved the child; for she was a kind-hearted woman, though she was sometimes cross.

"In a few minutes she went up to Nelly and took her bonnet off. Nelly submitted without a word. Then she made her a cup of tea; and while Nelly was taking it she asked her a great many questions. Nelly answered them all; and the landlady stared in amazement at the child's courage and resolution, and thought with herself.

"'Well, if anything can get Willie out of his bad ways, this little darling will do it.'

"Then she made her go to Willie's bed, promising to let her know the moment he came home.

"Nelly slept and slept till it was night. When she woke it was dark, but a light was shining through beneath the door. So she rose and put on her frock and shoes and stockings, and went to the kitchen.

"'You see he's not come yet, Nelly,' said the landlady.

"'Where can he be?' returned Nelly, sadly.

"'Oh! he'll be drinking with some of his companions in the public-house I suppose.'

"'Where is the public-house?'

"'There are hundreds of them, child.'

"'I know the place he generally goes to,' said a young tradesman who sat by the fire.

"He had a garret-room in the house, and knew Willie by sight. And he told the landlady in a low voice where it was.

"'Oh! do tell me, please sire,' cried Nelly. 'I want to get him home.'

"'You don't think he'll mind you, do you?'

"'Yes, I do,' returned Nelly confidently.

"'Well, I'll show you the way if you like; but you'll find it a rough place, I can tell you. You'll wish yourself out of it pretty soon, with or without Willie.'

"'I won't leave it without him,' said Nelly, tying on her bonnet.

"'Stop a bit,' said the landlady. 'You don't think I am going to let the child out with nobody but you to look after her?'

"'Come along, then, ma'am.'

"The landlady put on her bonnet, and out they all went into the street.

"What a wonder it *might* have been to Nelly! But she only knew that she was in the midst of great lights, and carts and carriages rumbling over the stones, and windows full of pretty things, and crowds of people jostling along the pavements. In all the show she wanted nothing but Willie.

"The young man led them down a long dark close through an archway, and then into a court off the close, and then up an outside stone stair to a low-browed door, at which he knocked.

"'I don't much like the look of this place,' said the landlady.

"Oh! there's no danger, I dare say, if you keep quiet. They'd never hurt the child. Besides, her brother'll see to that.'

"Presently the door was opened, and the young man asked after Willie.

"'Is he in?' he said.

"'He may be, or he may not,' answered a fat, frouzy woman, in a dirty cotton dress. 'Who wants him?'

"'This little girl.'

"'Please ma'am, I'm his sister.'

"'We want no sisters here.'

"And she proceeded to close the door. I dare say the landlady remembered with shame that that was just what she had done that morning.

"'Come! come!" interposed the young tradesman, putting his foot between the door and the post; 'don't be foolish. Surely you won't keep a child like that from speaking to her own brother! Why, the Queen herself would let her in.'

This softened the woman a little, and she hesitated, with the latch in her hand.

"'Mother wants him,' said Nelly. 'She's very ill. I heard her cry about Willie. Let me in.'

"She took hold of the woman's hand, who drew it away hastily, but stepped back at the same time, and let her enter. She then resumed her place at the door.

"'Devil a one of *you* shall come in!' she said, as if justifying the child's admission by the exclusion of the others.

"'We don't want, mistress,' said the young man. 'But we'll just see that no harm comes to her.'

"'D'ye think I'm not enough for that?' said the woman, with scorn. 'Let me see who dares to touch her! But you may stay where you are, if you like. The air's free.'

"So saying, she closed the door, with a taunting laugh.

"The passage was dark in which Nelly found herself; but she saw a light at the further end, through a keyhole, and heard the sounds of loud talk and louder laughter. Before the woman had closed the outer door, she had reached this room; nor did the woman follow either to guide or prevent her.

"A pause came in the noise. She tapped at the door.

"'Come in!' cried someone. And she entered.

"Round a table were seated four youths, drinking. Of them one was Willie, with flushed face and flashing eyes. They all stared when the child stood before them, in her odd, old-fashioned bonnet, and her little shawl pinned at the throat. Willie stared as much as any of them.

"Nelly spoke first.

"'Willie! Willie!' she cried, and would have rushed to him, but the table was between.

"'What do you want here, Nelly? Who the deuce let you come here?' said Willie, not quite unkindly.

"'I want you, Willie. Come home with me. Oh! please come home with me.'

"'I can't, now, Nelly, you see,' he answered. Then, turning to his companions, 'How could that child have found her way here?' he said, looking ashamed as he spoke.

"'You're fetched. That's all,' said one of them, with a sneer. 'Mother's sent for you.'

"'Go along!' said another; 'and mind you don't catch it when you get home!'

"'Nobody will say a word to you, Willie,' interposed Nelly.

"'Be a good boy, and don't do it again!' said the third, raising his glass to his lips.

"Willie tried to laugh, but was evidently vexed.

"'What are you standing there for, Nelly?' he said sharply. 'This is no place for you.'

"'Nor for you either, Willie,' returned Nelly, without moving.

"'We're all very naughty, aren't we, Nelly?' said the first.

"'Come and give me a kiss, and I'll forgive you,' said the second.

"'You shan't have your brother; so you may trudge home again without him,' said the third.

"And then all burst out laughing, except Willie.

"'Do go away, Nelly,' he said angrily.

"'Where am I to go to?' she asked.

"'Where you came from.'

"'That's home,' said Nelly; 'but I can't go home tonight, and I daren't go home without you. Mother would die. She's very ill, Willie. I heard her crying last night.'

"It seemed to Nelly at that moment that it was only last night she left home.

"'I'll just take the little fool to my lodgings and come back directly,' said Willie, rather stricken at this mention of his mother.

"Oh! yes. Do as you're bid!' they cried, and burst out laughing again. For they despised Willie because he was only a shepherd's son, although they liked to have his company because he was clever. But Willie was angry now.

"'I tell you what,' he said, 'I'll go when and where I like.'

"Two of them were silent now, because they were afraid of Willie; for he was big and strong. The third, however, trusting to the others, said, with a nasty sneer,

"'Go with its little sister to its little mammy!'

"Now Willie could not get out, so small was the room and so large the table, except one or other of those next to him rose to let him pass. Neither did. Willie therefore jumped on the table, kicked the tumbler of the one who had last spoken into the breast of his shirt, jumped down, took Nelly by the hand, and left the house.

"'The rude boys!' said Nelly. 'I would never go near them again, if I was you, Willie.'

"But Willie said never a word, for he was not pleased with Nelly, or with himself, or with his *friends*.

"When they got into the house he said abruptly. 'What's the matter with mother, Nelly?'

"'I don't know, Willie; but I don't think she'll ever get better. I'm sure father doesn't think it either.'

"Willie was silent for a long time. Then he said,

"'How did you come here, Nelly?'

"And Nelly told him the whole story.

"'And now you'll come home with me, Willie,'

"'It was very foolish of you, Nelly. To think you could bring me home if I didn't choose!'

"'But you do choose, don't you Willie?'

"'You might as well have written,' he said.

"Then Nelly remembered her father's letter, which the carrier had given her. And Willie took it, and sat down, with his back to Nelly, and read it through. Then he burst out crying, and lay his head on his arms and went on crying. And Nelly got upon a bar of the chair—for he was down on the table—and leaned over him, and put her arm round his neck, and said, crying herself all the time,

"'Nobody said a word to the black lamb when Jumper brought him home, Willie.'

"And Willie lifted his head, and put his arms round Nelly, and drew her face to his, and kissed her as he used to kiss her years ago.

"And I needn't tell you anything more about it."

"Oh! yes. Tell us how they got home."

"They went home with the carrier the next day."

"And wasn't his father glad to see Willie?"

"He didn't say much. He held out his hand with a half smile on his mouth, and a look in his eyes like the moon before a storm."

"And his mother?"

"His mother held out her arms, and drew him down to her bosom, and stroked his hair, and prayed God to bless Willie, her boy."

"And Nelly—weren't they glad to see Nelly?"

"They made more of Willie than they did of Nelly."

"And wasn't Nelly sorry?"

"No, she never noticed it—she was so busy making much of Willie, too."

"But I hope they didn't scold Nelly for going to fetch Willie?"

"When she went to bed that night, her father kissed her and said,

"'The blessin' o' an auld father be upo' ye, my wee bairn!'"

"There's Scotch." now exclaimed the whole company.

And in one moment papa was on the floor, buried beneath a mass of children.

The chief thumbsucker, after kissing till she was stupid, recovered her wits by sucking her thumb diligently for a whole minute, after which she said, "If we had been wolves, it would have been dangerous, papa."

And then they all went to bed.

Port in a Storm

"Papa," said my sister Effie, one evening as we all sat about the drawing-room fire. One after another, as nothing followed, we turned our eyes upon her. There she sat, still silent, embroidering the corner of a cambric handkerchief, apparently unaware that she had spoken.

It was a very cold night in the beginning of winter. My father had come home early, and we had dined early that we might have a long evening together, for it was my father's and mother's wedding-day, and we always kept it as the homeliest of holidays. My father was seated in an easy-chair by the chimney corner, with a jug of Burgundy near him, and my mother sat by his side, now and then taking a sip out of his glass.

Effie was now nearly nineteen; the rest of us were younger. What she was thinking about we did not know then, though we could all guess now. Suddenly she looked up, and seeing all eyes fixed upon her, became either aware or suspicious, and blushed rosy red.

"You spoke to me, Effie. What was it, my dear?"

"O yes, papa. I wanted to ask you whether you wouldn't tell us, to-night, the story about how you——"

"Well, my love?"

"——about how——"

"I am listening, my dear."

"I mean about mamma and you."

"Yes, yes. About how I got your mamma for a mother to you. Yes. I paid a dozen of port for her."

We all and each exclaimed *Papa!* and my mother laughed.

"Tell us about it," was the general cry.

"Well, I will," answered my father. "I must begin at the beginning, though."

And filling his glass with Burgundy, he began.

"As far back as I can remember, I lived with my father in an old manor-house in the country. It did not belong to my father, but to an elder brother of his, who at that time was captain of a seventy-four. He loved the sea more than his life; and, as yet apparently, had loved his ship better than any woman. At least he was not married.

"My mother had been dead for some years, and my father was now in very delicate health. He had never been strong, and since his mother's death, I believe, though I was too young to notice it, he had pined away.

I am not going to tell you anything about him just now, because it does not belong to my story. When I was about five years old, as nearly as I can judge, the doctors advised him to leave England. The house was put into the hands of an agent to let—at least, so I suppose; and he took me with him to Madeira, where he died. I was brought home by his servant, and by my uncle's directions, sent to a boarding-school; from there to Eton, and from there to Oxford.

"Before I had finished my studies, my uncle had been an admirable for some time. The year before I left Oxford, he married Lady Georgiana Thornbury, a widow lady, with one daughter. Thereupon he bade farewell to the sea, though I dare say he did not like the parting, and retired with his bride to the house where he was born—the same house I told you I was born in, which had been in the family for many generations, and which your cousin now lives in.

"It was late in the autumn when they arrived at Culverwood. They were no sooner settled than my uncle wrote me, inviting me to spend Christmas-tide with them at the old place. And here you may see my story has arrived at its beginning.

"It was with strange feelings that I entered the house. It looked so old-fashioned, and stately, and grand, to eyes which had been accustomed to all the modern commonplaces! Yet the shadowy recollections which hung about it gave an air of homeliness to the place, which, along with the grandeur, occasioned a sense of rare delight. For what can be better than to feel that you are in stately company, and at the same time perfectly at home in it? I am grateful to this day for the lesson I had from the sense of which I have spoken—that of mingled awe and tenderness in the aspect of the old hall as I entered it for the first time after fifteen years, having left it a mere child.

"I was cordially received by my old uncle and my new aunt. But the moment Kate Thornbury entered I lost my heart, and have never found it again to this day. I get on wonderfully well without it, though, for I have got the loan of a far better one till I find my own, which therefore, I hope I never shall."

My father glanced at my mother as he said this, and she returned his look in a way which I can now interpret as a quite satisfied confidence. But the tears came in Effie's eyes. She had trouble before long, poor girl! But it is not her story I have to tell.—My father went on:

"Your mother was prettier then than she is now, but not so beautiful; beautiful enough, though, to make me think there never had been or could again be anything so beautiful. She met me kindly, and I met her awkwardly."

"You made me feel that I had no business there," said my mother, speaking for the first time in the course of the story.

"See there, girls," said my father. "You are always so confidant in first impressions, and instinctive judgment! I was awkward because, as I said, I fell in love with your mother the moment I saw her; and she thought I regarded her as an intruder into the whole family precincts.

"I will not follow the story of the days. I was very happy, except when I felt too keenly how unworthy I was of Kate Thornbury; not that she meant to make me feel it, for she was never other than kind; but she was such that I could not help feeling it. I gathered, courage, however, and before three days were over, I began to tell her all my slowly reviving memories of the place, with my childish adventures associated with this and that room or outhouse or spot in the grounds; for the longer I was in the place the more my old associations with it revived, till I was quite astonished to find how much of my history in connection with Culverwood had been thoroughly imprinted on my memory. She never showed, at least, that she was weary of my stories; which, however interesting to me, must have been tiresome to any one who did not sympathize with what I felt towards my old nest. From room to room we rambled, talking or silent; and nothing could have given me a better chance, I believe, with a heart like your mother's. I think it was not long before she began to like me, at least, and liking had every opportunity of growing into something stronger, if only she too did not come to the conclusion that I was unworthy of her.

"My uncle received me like the jolly old tar that he was—welcomed me to the old ship—hoped we should make many a voyage together—and that I would take the run of the craft—all but in one thing.

"'You see, my boy,' he said, 'I married above my station, and I don't want my wife's friends to say that I laid alongside of her to get hold of her daughter's fortune. No, no, my boy; your old uncle has too much saltwater in him to do a dog's trick like that. So you take care of yourself—that's all. She might turn the head of a wiser man than ever came out of our family.'

"I did not tell my uncle that his advice was already too late; for that, though it was not an hour since I had first seen her, my head was so far turned already, that the only way to get it right again, was to go on turning it in the same direction; though, no doubt, there was a danger of overhauling the screw. The old gentleman never referred to the matter again, nor took any notice of our increasing intimacy; so that I sometimes doubt even now if he could have been in earnest in the very simple warning he gave me. Fortunately, Lady Georgiana liked me—at least I thought she did, and that gave me courage."

"That's all nonsense, my dear," said my mother, "Mamma was nearly as fond of you as I was; but you never wanted courage."

"I knew better than to show my cowardice, I dare say," returned my father, "But," he continued, "things grew worse and worse, till I was certain I should kill myself, to go straight out of my mind, if your mother would not have me. So it went on for a few days, and Christmas was at hand.

"The admirable had invited several friends to come and spend the Christmas week with him. Now you must remember that, although you look at me as an old-fashioned fogie——"

"Oh, papa!" we all interrupted; but he went on.

"Yet my old uncle was an older-fashioned fogie, and his friends were much the same as himself. Now, *I* am fond of a glass of port, though I dare not take it, and must content myself with Burgundy. Uncle Bob would have called Burgundy pig-wash. *He* could not do without his port, though he was a moderate enough man, as customs were. Fancy, then, his dismay when on questioning his butler, an old coxen of his own, and after going down to inspect in person, he found that there was scarcely more than a dozen of port in the wine-cellar. He turned white with dismay, and, till he had brought the blood back to his countenance by swearing, he was something awful to behold in the dim light of the tallow candle old Jacob held in his tattooed fist. I will not repeat the words he used; fortunately, they are out of fashion amongst gentlemen, although ladies, I understand, are beginning to revive the custom, now old, and always ugly. Jacob reminded his honour that he would not have more put down till he had a proper cellar built, for the one there was, he had said, was not fit to put anything but dead men in. Thereupon, after abusing Jacob for not reminding him of the necessities of the coming season, he turned to me, and began, certainly not to swear at his old father, but to expostulate sideways with the absent shade for not having provided a decent cellar before his departure from this world of dinners and wine, hinting that it was somewhat selfish, and very inconsiderate of the welfare of those who were to come after him. Having a little exhausted his indignation, he came up, and wrote the more peremptory order to his wine-merchant in Liverpool, to let him have thirty dozen of port before Christmas Day, even if he had to send it by port-chaise. I took the letter to the post office myself, for the old man would trust nobody but me, and indeed would have preferred taking it himself; but in winter he was always lame from the effects of a bruise he had received from a falling spar in the battle of Aboukir.

"That night I remember well. I lay in bed wondering whether I might say a word, or even to give a hint to your mother that there was a word that pined to be said if it might. All at once I heard a whine! For my kind aunt had taken the trouble to find out what room I had occupied as a boy, and, by the third night I spent there, she had got it ready for me. I jumped out of bed, and found that the snow was falling fast and thick. I jumped into bed again, and began wondering what my uncle would do if the port did not arrive. And then I thought that, if the snow went on falling as it did, and if the wind rose any higher, it might turn out that the roads through the hilly part of Yorkshire in which Culverwood lay, might very well be blocked up.

> "*The north wind doth blow,*
> *And we shall have snow,*
> *An what shall my uncle do then, poor thing?*
> *He'll run for his port,*
> *But he shall run short,*
> *And have too much water to drink, poor thing!*

"With the influence of the chamber of my childhood, I kept repeating the travestied rhyme to myself, till I fell asleep.

"Now, boys and girls, if I were writing a novel, I should like to make you, somehow or other, gather the facts—that I was in the room I mentioned; that I had been in the cellar with my uncle for the first time that evening; that I had seen my uncle's distress, and heard his reflections upon his father. I may add that I was not myself, even then, so indifferent to the merits of a good glass of port as to be unable to enter into my uncle's dismay, and that his guests at last, if they had found that the snowstorm had actually closed up the sweet approach of the expected port. If I was personally indifferent too the matter, I fear it is to be attributed to your mother, and not to myself."

"Nonsense!" interposed my mother once more. "I never knew such a man for making little of himself and much of other people. You never drank a glass too much of port in your life."

"That's why I'm so fond of it, my dear," returned my father. "I declare you make me quite discontented with my pig-wash here.

"That night I had a dream.

"The next day the visitors began to arrive. Before the evening after, they had all come. There were five of them—three tars and two land-crabs, as they called each other when they got jolly, which, by-the-way, they would not have done long without me.

"My uncle's anxiety visibly increased. Each guest, as he came down to breakfast, received each morning a more constrained greeting.—I beg your pardon, ladies; I forgot to mention that my aunt had lady-visitors, of course. But the fact is, it is only the port-drinking visitors in whom my story is interested, always excepted your mother.

"These ladies my admirable uncle greeted with something even approaching servility. I understood him well enough. He instinctively sought to make a party to protect him when the awful secret of his cellar should be found out. But for two preliminary days or so, his resources would serve; for he had plenty of excellent claret and Madiera—stuff I don't know much about—and both Jacob and himself condescended to manoeuver a little.

"The wine did not arrive. But the morning of Christmas Eve did. I was sitting in my room, trying to write a song for Kate—that's your mother, my dears——"

"I know, papa," said Effie, as if she was very knowing to know that.

"——when my uncle came into the room, looking like Sintram with Death and the Other One after him—that's the nonsense you read to me the other day, isn't it Effie?"

"Not nonsense, dear papa," remonstrated Effie; and I loved her for saying it, for surely *that* is not nonsense.

"I didn't mean it," said my father; and turning to my mother, added: "It must be your fault, my dear, that my children are so serious that they always take a joke for earnest. However, it was no joke with my uncle. If he didn't look like Sintram he looked like t'other one.

"'The roads are frozen— I mean snowed up,' he said. 'There's just one bottle of port left, and what Captain Calker will say—, I dare say I know, but I'd rather not. Damn this weather!—God forgive me!—that's not right—but it *is* trying—ain't it, my boy?'

"'What will you give me for a dozen of port, uncle?'

"'Give you? I'll give you Culverwood, you rogue.'

"'Done,' I cried.

"'That is,' stammered my uncle, 'that is,' and he reddened like the funnel of one of his hated steamers, 'that is, you know, always provided, you know. It wouldn't be fair to Lady Georgiana, now would it? I put it to yourself—if she took the trouble, you know. You understand me, my boy?'

"'That's of course, uncle,' I said.

"'Ah! I see you're a gentleman like your father, not to trip a man when he stumbles,' said my uncle. For such was the old man's sense of honour that he was actually uncomfortable about the hasty promise he had made without first specifying the exception. The exception, you know, has Culverwood at the present hour, and right welcome he is.

"'Of course, uncle,' I said—between gentlemen, you know. Still, I want my joke out, too. What will you give me for a dozen of port to tide you over Christmas Day?'

"'Give you, my boy? I'll give you——'

"But here he checked himself, as one that has been burned already.

"'Bah!' he said, turning his back, and going towards the door; 'what's the use of joking about serious affairs like this?'

"And so he left the room. And I let him go. For I had heard that the road from Liverpool was impassible, the wind and the snow having continued every day since the night of which I told you. Meantime, I had never been able to summon the courage to say one word to your mother—I beg your pardon, I mean Miss Thornbury.

"Christmas Day arrived. My uncle was awful to behold. His friends were evidently anxious about him. They thought he was ill. There was such a hesitation about him, like a sharp hook with a bait, and such a flurry, like a whale in his last agonies. He had a horrible secret which he dared not tell, and yet *would* come out of its grave at the appointed hour.

"Down in the kitchen the roast beef and turkey were meeting their deserts. Up in the store-room—for Lady Georgiana was not above housekeeping, any more than her daughter—the ladies of the house were doing their part; and I was oscillating between my uncle and his niece, making myself amazingly useful now to one and now to the other. The turkey and the beef were on the table, nay, they had been well eaten, before I felt that my moment was come. Outside, the wind was howling, and driving the snow with soft pats against the window-pane. Eager-eyed I watched General Fortescue, who despised sherry or Madeira even during dinner, and would no more touch champagne than he would *eau secrèe*, but drank port after fish or with cheese indiscriminately—with eager eyes I watched how the last bottle dwindled out of its fading life in the clear decanter. Glass after glass was supplied to General Fortescue by the fearless cockswain, who, if he might have his choice, would rather have boarded a Frenchman than waited for what was to follow. My uncle scarcely ate at all, and the only thing that stopped his face from growing longer with the removal of every dish was that nothing but death could have made it longer than it was already. It was my interest to let matters go as far as they might up to a certain point, beyond which it was not my interest to let them go, if I could help it. At the same time I was curious to know how my uncle would announce—confess the terrible fact that in his house, on Christmas Day, having invited his oldest friends to share with him the festivities of the season, there was not one bottle of port to be had.

"I waited till the last moment—till I fancied the admirable was opening his mouth, like a fish in despair, to make his confession. He had not even dared to make a confidante of his wife in such an awful dilemma. Then I pretended to have dropped my table-napkin behind my chair, and rising to seek it stole round behind my uncle, and whispered in his ear:

"'What will you give for a dozen of port now, uncle?'

"'Bah!' he said, 'I'm at the gratings; don't torture me.'

"'I'm in earnest, uncle.'

"He looked round at me with a sudden flash of bewildered hope in his eye. In the last agony he was capable of believing in a miracle. But he made me no reply. He only stared.

"'Will you give me Kate?' I want Kate," I whispered

"'I will, my boy. That is, if she'll have you. That is, I mean to say, if you produce the true tawny.'

"'Of course, uncle; honour bright—as port in a storm,' I answered, trembling in my shoes and everything else I had on, for I was not more than three times confidant in the result.

"The gentlemen beside Kate happening at the moment to be occupied, each with the lady on his other side, I went behind her, and whispered to her as I had whispered to my uncle, though not exactly in the same terms. Perhaps I had got a little courage from the champagne I had drunk; perhaps the excitement of the whole venture kept me up; perhaps Kate herself gave me courage, like a goddess of old in some way I did not understand. At all events I said to her—

"'Kate,'—we had not got so far even then—'my uncle hasn't another bottle of port in his cellar. Consider what a state General Fortescue will be in soon. He'll be tipsy for want of it. Will you come and help me to find a bottle or two?'

"She rose at once, with a white-rose blush—so delicate. I don't believe anyone saw it but myself. But the shadow of a stray ringlet could not fall on her cheek without my seeing it.

"When we got into the hall, the wind was roaring loud, and a few lights were flickering and waving gustingly with alternate light and shade across the old portraits which I had known so well as a child—for I used to think what each would say first, if he or she came down out of the frame and spoke to me."

"I stopped, and taking Kate's hand I said—

"'I daren't let you come farther, Kate, before I tell you another thing: my uncle has promised, if I find him a dozen of port—you must have seen what state the poor man is in—to let me say something to you—I suppose he meant your mamma, but I prefer saying it to you, if you will let me. Will you come and help me find the port?'

"She said nothing, but took the candle that was on a table in the hall. I ventured to look at her. Her face was now a celestial rosy red, and I could not doubt that she understood me. She looked so beautiful that I stood staring at her without moving. What the servants could have been about that not one of them crossed the hall, I can't think.

"At last Kate laughed and said—'Well.' I started, and I dare say took my turn at blushing. At least I did not know what to say. I had forgotten all about the guests inside. 'Where's the port?' said Kate. I caught hold of her hand again and kissed it."

"You needn't be quite so minute in your account, my dear," said my mother, smiling.

"I will be more careful in the future, my love," returned my father.

"'What do you want me to do?' said Kate.

"'Only to hold the candle for me,' I answered, restored to my seven senses at last; and taking it from her, I led the way, and she followed, till we had passed through the kitchen and reached the cellar-stairs. These were steep and awkward, and she let me help her down."

"Now, Edward!" said my mother.

"Yes, yes, my love, I understand," returned my father.

"Up to this time your mother had asked no questions, but when we stood in a vast low cellar, which we had made several turns to reach it, and I gave her the candle, and took up a great crowbar which lay on the floor, she said at last—

"'Edward are you going to bury me alive? or what *are* you going to do?'

"'I'm going to dig you out,' I said, for I was nearly beside myself with joy, as I struck the crowbar like a battering-ram into the wall. You can fancy, John, that I didn't work the worse that Kate was holding the candle for me.

"Very soon, though with great effort, I had dislodged a brick, and the next blow I gave into the hole sent back a dull echo. I was right!

"I worked now like a madman, and, in a very few minutes more, I had dislodged the whole of the brick-thick wall which filled up an archway of stone and curtained an ancient door in the lock of which the key now showed itself. It had been well greased, and I turned it without much difficulty.

"I took the candle of Kate and led her into a specious region of sawdust, cobweb, and wine-fungus. "'There, Kate!' I cried, in delight.

"'But,' said Kate, 'will the wine be good?'

"'General Fortescue will answer you that,' I replied exultantly. 'Now come, and hold the light again while I find the port-bin.'

"I soon found not one, but several wine-filled port-bins. What to choose I could not tell. I must chance that Kate carried a bottle and a candle, and I carried two bottles very carefully. We put them down in the kitchen with orders that they should not be touched. We had soon carried the dozen to the hall-table very carefully.

"When at length, with Jacob chuckling and running his hands behind us, we entered the dining-room, Kate and I, for Kate would not part with her share in the business, loaded with a level bottle in each hand, which we carefully erected on the sideboard, I presume, from the stare of the company, that we presented a rather remarkable appearance—Kate in her white muslin and I in my best clothes, covered with brick-dust, and cobwebs, and lime. But we could not be half so amusing to them as they were to us. There they sat with the dessert before them, but no wine-decanters forthcoming. How long they had sat thus, I have no idea. If you think your mamma has, you may ask her. Captain Calker and General Fortescue looked positively white about the gills. My uncle, clinging to the last hope, despairingly, had sat still and said nothing, and the guests could not understand the awful delay. Even Lady Georgiana had begun to fear a mutiny in the kitchen, or something equally awful. But to see the flash that passed across my uncle's face, when he saw us appear with *ported arms!* He immediately began to pretend that nothing had been the matter.

"'What the deuce has kept you, Ned, my boy?' he said. 'Fair Hebe,' he went on, 'I beg your pardon. Jacob, you can go on decanting. It was very careless of you to forget it. Meantime, Hebe, bring that bottle to General Jupiter, there. He's got a corkscrew in the tail of his robe, or I'm mistaken.'

"Out came General Fortescue's corkscrew. I was trembling more with anxiety. The cork gave the genuine plop; the bottle was lowered; glug, glug, glug, came from its beneficent throat, and out flowed something as tawny as a lion's mane. The general lifted it lazily to his lips, saluting his nose on the way.

"'Fifteen by Gyeove!' he cried. 'Well, Admirable, this *was* worth waiting for! Take care now you decant that, Jacob—on peril of your life.'

My uncle was triumphant. He winked hard at me not to tell. Kate and I retired, she to change her dress, I to get mine well brushed, and my hands washed. By the time I returned to the dining-room, no one had any questions to ask. For Kate, the ladies had gone to the drawing room before she was ready, and I believe she had some difficulty keeping my uncle's counsel. But she did.—Need I say that was the happiest Christmas I ever spent?"

"But how did you find the cellar, papa?" asked Effie.

"Where are your brains Effie? Don't you remember I told you I had a dream?"

"Yes. But you don't mean to say the existence of a wine-cellar was revealed to you in a dream?"

"But I do indeed. I had seen the wine-cellar built up just before we left for Madeira. It was my father's plan for securing the wine when the house was let. And very well it turned out for the wine, and me too. I had forgotten all about it. Everything had conspired to bring it to my memory, but had just failed of success. I had fallen asleep under all the influences I told you of—influences from the region of my childhood. They operated still when I was asleep, and, all other distracting influences being removed, at length, roused in my sleeping brain the memory of what I had seen. In the morning I remembered not my dream only, but the event of which my dream was a reproduction. Still, I was under considerable doubt about the place, and in this I followed the dream only, as near as I could judge.

"The admirable kept his word, and interposed no difficulties between Kate and me. Not that, to tell the truth, I was ever anxious about that rock ahead; but it was very possible that his fastidious honor or pride might have occasioned a considerable interference with our happiness for a time. As it turned out, he could not leave me Culverwood, and I regretted the fact as little as he did himself. His gratitude to me was, however, excessive, assuming occasionally ludicrous outbursts of thankfulness. I do not believe he could have been more grateful if I had saved his ship and its whole crew. For his hospitality was at stake. Kind old man!"

Here ended my father's story, with a light sigh, a gaze into the bright coals, a kiss of my mother's hand which he held in his, and another glass of Burgundy.

The Gifts of the Child Christ

CHAPTER I

"My hearers, we grow old," said the preacher. "Be it summer or be it spring with us now, autumn will soon settle down into winter, that winter whose snow melts only in the grave. The wind of the world sets for the tomb. Some of us rejoice to be swept along on swift wings, and hear it bellowing in the hollows of earth and sky; but it will grow a terror to the man of trembling limbs and withered brain, until at length he will long for the shelter of the tomb to escape its roaring and buffeting. Happy the man who shall then be able to believe that old age itself, with its pitiable decays and sad dreams of youth, is the chastening of the Lord, a sure sign of his love and fatherhood."

It was the first Sunday in Advent; but "the chastening of the Lord" came into almost every sermon that man preached.

"Eloquent! But after all, *can* this thing be true?" said to himself a man about thirty, who sat decorously listening. For many years he had thought he believed this kind of thing—but of late he was not so sure.

Beside him his wife, in her new winter bonnet, her pretty face turned up toward the preacher; but her eyes—nothing else—revealed that she was not listening. She was much younger than her husband—hardly twenty, indeed.

In the upper corner of the pew sat a pale-faced child about five, sucking her thumb, and staring at the preacher.

The sermon over, they walked home in proximity. The husband looked gloomy, and his eyes sought the ground. The wife looked more smiling than cheerful, and her pretty eyes went hither and thither. Behind them walked the child—steadily, "with level-fronting eyelids."

It was a late-built region of large, commonplace houses, and at one of them they stopped and entered. The door of the dining-room was open, showing the table laid for their Sunday dinner. The gentleman passed on to the library behind it, the lady went up to her bedroom, and the child a stage higher to the nursery.

It was half an hour to dinner. Mr. Greatorex sat down, drummed with his fingers on the arm of his easy-chair, took up a book of arctic exploration, threw it again on the table, got up, and went to the smoking-room. He had built it for his wife's sake, but was often glad of it for his own. Again he seated himself, took a cigar and smoked gloomily.

Having reached her bedroom, Mrs. Greatorex took off her bonnet, and stood for ten minutes turning it round and round. Earnestly she regarded it—now gave a twist to the wire-stem of a flower, then spread wider the loop of a bow. She was meditating what it lacked of perfection rather than brooding over its merits: she was keen in bonnets.

Little Sophy—or, as she called herself by a transposition of consonants common with children, Phosy—found her nurse Alice in the nursery. But she was lost in the pages of a certain London weekly, which had found her in a mood open to its influences, and did not even look up when the child entered. With some effort Phosy drew off her gloves, and with more difficulty untied her hat. Then she took off her jacket, smoothed her hair, and retreated to a corner. There a large shabby doll lay upon her chair: she took it up, disposed it gently on the bed, got a little book from where she had left it under the chair, smoothed down her skirts, and began simultaneously to read and suck her thumb. The book was an unhealthy one: a cup filled to the brim with a poverty-stricken and selfish religion: such are always breaking out like an eruption here and there over the body of the Church, doing their part, doubtless, in carrying off the evil rumours generated by poverty of blood, or the congestion of self-preservation. It is wonderful out of what spoiled fruit some children will suck sweetness.

But she did not read far: her thoughts went back to a phrase which had haunted her ever since first she went to church: "Whom the Lord loveth, he chasteneth."

"I wish he would chasten me," she thought for the hundredth time.

The small Christian had no suspicion that her whole life had been a period of chastening—that few children indeed have to live in such a sunless atmosphere as hers.

Alice threw down the newspaper, gazed from the window into the back-yard of the next house, saw nothing but an elderly man-servant brushing a garment, and turned to Sophy.

"Why don't you hang up your jacket, miss?" she said, sharply.

The little one rose, opened the wardrobe-door wide, carried her chair to it, fetched the jacket from her bed, clambered up on the chair, and leaning forward to reach a peg, tumbled right into the bottom of the wardrobe.

"You clumsy!" exclaimed the nurse angrily, and pulling her out by the arm, shook her.

Alice was not generally rough to her, but there were reasons to-day.

Phosy crept back to her seat, pale, frightened, and a little hurt. Alice hung up the jacket, closed the wardrobe, and, turning, contemplated her own pretty face and neat figure in the glass opposite, The dinner-bell rang.

"There, I declare!" she cried, and wheeled around on Phosy. "And your hair not brushed yet, miss! Will you ever learn to do a thing without being told it? Thank goodness I shan't be plagued with you long! But I pity her as comes after me, I do!"

"If the Lord would but chasten me!" said the child to herself, as she laid down her book with a sigh.

The maid seized her roughly by the arm, and brushed her hair with an angry haste that made the child's eyes water, and herself feel a little ashamed at the sight of them.

"How could anyone love such a troublesome chit?" she said, seeking the comfort of justification from the child herself.

Another sigh was the poor little damsel's only answer. She looked very white and solemn as she entered the dining-room.

Mr. Greatorex was a merchant in the City. But he was more of a man than a merchant, which all merchants are not. Also, he was more scrupulous in his dealings than some merchants in the same line of business, who yet stood as well with the world as he, but on the other hand, he had the meanness to pride himself upon it as if it had been something he might have done without and yet held up his head.

Some six years before, he was married to please his parents; and a year before, he had married to please himself. His first wife had intellect, education, and heart, but little individuality—not enough to reflect the individuality of her husband. The consequence was, he found her uninteresting. He was kind and indulgent, however, and not even her best friend blamed him much for manifesting nothing beyond the average devotion of husbands. But in truth his wife had great capabilities, only they had never ripened, and when she died, a fortnight after giving birth to Sophy, her husband had not a suspicion of the large amount of undeveloped power that had passed away with her.

Her child was so like both in countenance and manner that he was too constantly reminded of her unlamented mother; and he loved neither enough to discover that, in a sense as true as marvellous, the child was the very flower-bud of her mother's nature, in which her retarded blossom had yet a chance of being slowly carried to perfection. Love alone gives insight, and her father took her merely for a miniature edition of the volume which he seemed to have laid aside forever. Instead, therefore, of watering the roots of his little human slip from the wells of his affections, he had scarcely as yet perceived more in relation to her than that he was legally accountable for her existence, and bound to give her shelter and food. If he had questioned himself on the matter, he would have replied that love was not wanting, only waiting upon her growth, and the development of something to interest him.

Little right as he had to expect anything from his first marriage, he had yet cherished some hopes therein—intolerably vague, it is true, yet hardly faint enough, it would seem, for he was disappointed in them. When its bonds fell from him, however, he flattered himself that he had not worn them in vain, but had through them arrived at a knowledge of women as rare as profound. But whatever the reach of this knowledge, it was not sufficient to prevent him from harbouring the presumptuous hope of so choosing and so fashioning the heart and mind of a woman that they should be as concave mirrors of his own. I do not mean that he would have admitted the figure, but such was really the end he blindly sought. I wonder how many of those who have been disappointed in such an attempt have been thereby aroused to the perception of what a frightful failure their success would have been on both sides. It was bad enough that Augustus Greatorex's theories had cramped his own development; it would have been ten-fold worse had they been operative to the stunting of another soul.

Letty Merewether was the daughter of a bishop *in partibus.* She had been born tolerably innocent, had grown up more than tolerably pretty, and was, when she came to England at the age of sixteen, as nearly a genuine example of Locke's sheet of white paper as could have fallen to the hand of such an experimenter as Greatorex would fain become.

In his suit he had prospered—perhaps too easily. He loved the girl, or at least loved the modified reflection of her in his own mind; while she, thoroughly admiring the dignity, good looks, accomplishments of the man whose attention flattered her self-opinion, accorded him deference enough to encourage his vainest hopes. Although she knew little, fluttered over the merest surfaces of existence, she had sense enough to know that he talked sense to her, and foolishness enough to put it down to her own credit, while for the sense itself she cared little or nothing. And Greatorex, without even knowing what she was roughhewn for, would take upon him to shape her ends!—an ambition the Divinity never permits to succeed: he who fancies himself the carver finds himself but the chisel, or indeed perhaps only the mallet, in the hand of the true workman.

During the days of courtship, then, Letty listened and smiled, or answered with what he took for a spiritual response, when it was merely a brain-echo. Looking down into the pond of her being, whose surface was not yet ruffled by any bubbling of springs from below, he saw the reflection of himself and was satisfied. An able man on his hobby looks a centaur of wisdom and folly; but if he be at all a wise man, the beast will one day or other show him the jade's favour of unseating him. Meantime Augustus Greatorex was fooled, not by poor little Letty, who was not capable of fooling him, but by himself. Letty had made no pretences; had been interested, and had shown her interest; had understood, or seemed to understand, what he said to her, and forgotten it the next moment—had no pocket to put it in, did not know what to do with it, and let it drop into the Limbo of Vanity. They had not been married many days before the scouts of advancing disappointment were upon them. Augustus resisted manfully for a time. But the truth was each of the two had to become a great deal more than either was, before any approach to unity was possible. He tried to interest her in one subject after another—tried her first, I am ashamed to say, with political economy. In that instance, when he came home to dinner he found that she had not got past the first page of the book he had left with her. But she had the best of excuses, namely, that of that page she had not understood a sentence. He saw his mistake, and tried her with poetry. But Milton, with whom unfortunately he had commenced his approaches, was to her, if not equally unintelligible, equally uninteresting. He tried her next with elements of science, but with no better success. He returned to poetry, and read some of the *Faerie Queene* with her: she was, or seemed to be, interested in all his talk about it, and inclined to go on with it in his absence, but found the first stanza she tried more than enough without him to give life to it. She could give it none, and therefore it gave her none. I believe she read a chapter of the Bible every day, but the only books she read with real interest were novels of a sort Augustus despised. It never occurred to him that he ought at once to have made friends of this Momus of unrighteousness, for by it he might have found entrance to the sealed chamber. He ought to have read with her the books she did like, for by them only could he make her think, and from them alone could he lead her to better. It is but from the very step upon which one stands that one can move to the next. Besides these books, there was nothing in the scheme of her universe but fashion, dress, calls, the park, other-peopledom, concerts, plays, church-going—whatever could show itself on the frosted glass of her *camera obscura*—make an interest of motion and colour on her darkened chamber. Without these, her bosom's mistress would have found life unendurable, for not yet had she ascended her throne, but lay on the floor of her nursery, surrounded with toys that imitated life.

It was no wonder therefore that Augustus was at length compelled to allow himself disappointed. That it was the fault of his self-confidence made the thing no whit better. He was too much a man not to cherish certain tenderness for her, but he soon found to his dismay that it had begun to be mingled with a shadow of contempt. Against this he struggled, but with fluctuating success. He stopped later and later at business, and when he came home spent more and more of his time in the smoking room, where by and by he had bookshelves put up. Occasionally he would accept an invitation to dinner and accompany his wife, but he detested evening parties, and when Letty, who never refused an invitation if she could help it, went to one, he remained at home with his books. But his power of reading began to diminish. He became restless and irritable. Something kept gnawing at his heart. There was a sore spot in it. The spot grew larger and larger, and by degrees the centre of his consciousness came to be a soreness; his cherished idea had been fooled; he had taken a silly girl for a woman of undeveloped wealth;—a bubble, a surface whereon fair colours chased each other, for a hearted crystal.

On her part, Letty too had her grief, which, unlike Augustus, she did not keep to herself, receiving in return from one of her friends the soothing assurance that Augustus was only like all other men; that women were but their toys, which they cast away when weary of them. Letty did not see that she herself was making a toy of her life, or that Augustus was right in refusing to play with such a costly and delicate thing. Neither did Augustus see that, having, by his own blunder, married a mere child, he was bound to deal with her as one, and not let the child suffer for his fault more than could not be helped. It is not by pressing our insights upon them, but by bathing the sealed eyelids of the human kittens, that we can help them.

And all the time poor little Phosy was left to the care of Alice, a clever, useless, good-hearted, self-satisfied damsel, who, although seldom so rough in her behaviour as we have just seen her, abandoned the child almost entirely to her own resources. It was often she sat alone in the nursery, wishing the Lord would chasten her—because then he would love her.

The first course was nearly over ere Augustus had brought himself to ask—

"What did you think of the sermon today, Letty?"

"Not much," answered Letty. "I am not fond of finery. I prefer simplicity."

Augustus held his peace bitterly. For it was just finery in a sermon, without knowing it, that Letty was fond of: what seemed to him a flimsy syllabub of sacred things, beaten up with the whisk of composition, was charming to Letty; while on the contrary, if a man such as they been listening to was carried away by the thoughts that struggle in him for utterance, the result, to her judgment, was finery, and the object display. In excuse it must be remembered that she had been used to her father's style, which no one could have aspersed with lack of sobriety.

Presently she spoke again.

"Gus, dear, couldn't you make up your mind for once to go with me to Lady Ashdaile's to-morrow? I am quite ashamed of appearing so often without you."

"There is another way of avoiding that unpleasantness," remarked her husband drily.

"You cruel creature!" returned Letty playfully. "But I must go this once, for I promised Mrs. Holden."

"You know, Letty," said her husband, after a little pause, "it gets of more and more consequence that you should not fatigue yourself. By keeping such late hours in such stifling rooms you are endangering two lives—remember that, Letty. If you stay at home tomorrow, I will come home early, and read to you all the evening."

"Gussy, that *would* be charming. You *know* there is nothing in the world I should enjoy so much. But this time I really mustn't."

She launched into a list of all the great nobodies and small somebodies who were to be there, and whom she positively must see: it might be her only chance.

Those last words quenched a sarcasm on Augustus' lips. He was kinder than usual the rest of the evening, and read her to sleep with the Pilgrim's Progress.

Phosy sat in a corner, listened, and understood. Or where she misunderstood, it was an honest misunderstanding, which never does much hurt. Neither father nor mother spoke to her till they bade her good night. Neither saw the hungry heart under the mask of the still face. The father never imagined her already fit for the modelling she was better without, and the stepmother had to become a mother before she could value her.

Phosy went to bed to dream of the Valley of Humiliation.

CHAPTER II

The next morning Alice gave her mistress warning. It was quite unexpected, and she looked at her aghast.

"Alice," she said at length, "you're never going to leave me at such a time!"

"I'm sorry it don't suit you, ma'am, but I must."

"Why, Alice? What is the matter? Has Sophy been troublesome?"

"No, ma'am, there's no harm in that child."

"Then what can it be, Alice? Perhaps you are going to be married sooner that you expected?"

Alice gave her chin a little toss, pressed her lips together, and was silent.

"I have always been kind to you," resumed her mistress.

"I'm sure, ma'am, I never made no complaints!" returned Alice, but as she spoke she drew herself up straighter than before.

"Then what is it?" said her mistress.

"The fact is, ma'am," answered the girl, almost fiercely, "I can*not* any longer endure a state of domestic slavery."

"I don't understand you a bit better," said Mrs. Greatorex, trying, but in vain, to smile, and therefore looking angrier than she was.

"I mean ma'am—an' I see no reason I shouldn't say it, for it's the truth—there's a worm at the root of society where one yuman bein's got to do the dirty work of another. I don't mind sweepin' up my own dust, but I wont sweep up nobody else's. I ain't a goin' to demean myself no longer! There!"

"Leave the room, Alice," said Mrs. Greatorex; and when, with a toss and a flounce, the young woman had vanished, she burst into tears of anger and annoyance.

The day passed. The evening came. She dressed without Alice's usual help, and went to Lady Ashdaile's with her friend. There a reaction took place, and her spirits rose unnaturally. She even danced—to the disgust of one or two quick-eyed matrons who sat by the wall.

When she came home she found her husband sitting up for her. He said next to nothing, and sat up an hour longer with his book.

In the night she was taken ill. Her husband called Alice, and ran himself to fetch the doctor. For some hours she seemed in danger, but by noon was much better. Only the greatest care was necessary.

As soon as she could speak, she told Augustus of Alice's warning, and he sent for her to the library.

She stood before him with flushed cheeks and flashing eyes.

"I understand, Alice, you have given your mistress warning," he said gently.

"Yes, sir."

"Don't you think it would be ungrateful of you to leave her in her present condition? She's not likely to be strong for some time to come."

The use of the word "ungrateful" was an unfortunate one. Alice begged to know what she had to be grateful for. Was her work worth nothing? And her master, as everyone must who claims that which can only be freely given, found himself in the wrong.

"Well, Alice," he said, "we won't dispute that point; and if you are really determined on going, you must do the best you can for your mistress for the rest of the month."

Alice's sense of injury was soothed by her master's forbearance. She had always rather approved of Mr. Greatorex, and she left the room more softly than she had entered it.

Letty had a fortnight in bed, during which she reflected a little.

The very next day on which she left her room, Alice sought an interview with her master, and declared she could not stay out the month; she must go home at once.

She had been very attentive to her mistress during the fortnight: there must be something to account for her strange behaviour.

"Come now, Alice," said her master, "what's at the back of all this? You have been a good, well-behaved. obliging girl till now, and I am certain you would never be like this if there weren't something wrong somewhere."

"Something wrong, sir! No, indeed, sir! Except you call it wrong to have an old uncle who dies and leaves ever so much money—thousands on thousands, the lawyers say."

"And does it come to you then, Alice?"

"I get my share, sir. He left it to be parted even between his nephews and nieces."

"Why, Alice, you are quite an heiress, then!" returned her master, scarcely, however, believing the thing so grand as Alice would have it. "But don't you think now it would be rather hard that your fortune should be Mrs. Greatorex's misfortune?"

"Well, I don't see how it shouldn't." replied Alice. "It's mis'ess's fortun' as 'as been my misfortun'—ain't it now, sir? An' why shouldn't it be the other way next?"

"I don't quite see how your mistress's fortune can be said to be your misfortune, Alice."

"Anybody would see that, sir, as wasn't blinded by class-prejudices."

"Class-prejudices!" exclaimed Mr. Greatorex, in surprise at the word.

"It's a term they use, I believe, sir! But it's plain enough that if mis'ess hadn't 'a' been better off than me, she wouldn't ha' been able to secure my services—as you calls it."

"That is certainly plain enough," returned Mr. Greatorex. "But suppose nobody had been able to secure your services, what would have become of you?"

"By that time the people'd have arose to assert their rights."

"To what?—To fortunes like yours?"

"To bread and cheese at least, sir," returned Alice pertly.

"Well, but you've had something better than bread and cheese."

"I don't make no complaints as to the style of livin' in the house, sir, but that's all one, so long as it's on the vile condition of domestic slavery—which it's nothing can justify."

"Then of course, although you are now a woman of property, you will never dream of having any one to wait on you," said her master, amused with the volume of human nature thus opened to him.

"All I say, sir, is—it's my turn now; and I ain't goin' to sit upon by no one. I know my dooty to myself."

"I didn't know there was such a duty, Alice," said her master.

Something in his tone displeased her.

"Then you know now, sir," she said, and bounced out of the room.

The next moment, however, ashamed of her rudeness, she re-entered, saying,

"I don't want to be unkind, sir, but I must go home. I've got a brother that's ill, too, and wants to see me. If you don't object to me goin' home for a month, I promise you to come back and see mis'ess through her trouble—as a friend, you know, sir."

"But just listen to me first, Alice," said Mr. Greatorex. "I've had something to do with wills in my time, and I can assure you it is not likely to be less than a year before you can touch the money. You had much better stay where you are till your uncle's affairs are settled. You don't know what may happen. There's many a slip between cup and lip, you know."

"Oh! it's all right, sir. Everybody knows the money's left to his nephews and nieces, and me and my brother's as good as any."

"I don't doubt it: still, if you'll take my advice, you'll keep a sound roof over your head till another's ready for you."

Alice only threw her chin in the air, and said almost threatening,

"Am I to go for the month, sir?"

"I'll talk to your mistress about it," answered Mr. Greatorex, not at all sure that such an arrangement would be to his wife's comfort.

But the next day Mrs. Greatorex had a long talk with Alice, and the result was that on the following Monday she was to go home for a month, and then return for two months more at least. What Mr. Greatorex had said about the legacy, had had its effect, and, besides, her mistress had spoken to her with pleasure in her good fortune. About Sophy no one felt any anxiety: she was no trouble to any one, and the housemaid would see to her.

CHAPTER III

On the Sunday evening, Alice's lover, having heard, not from herself, but by a side wind, that she was going home the next day, made his appearance in Wimborne Square, somewhat perplexed—both at the move, and at her leaving him in ignorance of the same. He was a cabinet maker in an honest shop in the neighbourhood, and in education, faculty, and general worth, considerably Alice's superior,—a fact which had hitherto rather pleased her, but now gave zest to the change which she imagined had subverted their former relation. Full of the sense of her new superiority, she met him draped in an indescribable strangeness. John Jephson felt, at the very first word, as if her voice came from the other side of the English Channel. He wondered what he had done, or rather what Alice could imagine he had done or said, to put her in such tantrums.

"Alice, my dear," he said—for John was a man to go straight at the enemy, "what's amiss? What's come over you? You ain't altogether like your own self to-night! And here I find you goin' away, and ne'er a word to me about it! What have I done?"

Alice's chin made reply. She waited the fitting moment, with splendour to astonish, and with grandeur to subdue her lover. To tell the sad truth, she was no longer sure that it would be well to encourage him on the old footing; on the brink of the brook that parted serfdom from gentility, on the point of stepping daintily across, and leaving domestic slavery, red hands, caps, and obedience behind her? How then was she to marry a man that had black nails, and smelt of glue? It was incumbent on her at least, for propriety's sake, to render him at once aware that it was in condescension ineffable she took any notice of him.

"Alice, my girl!" began John again, in expostulatory tone.

"Miss Cox, if you please, John Jephson," interposed Alice.

"What on 'arth's come over you?" exclaimed John, with the first throb of rousing indignation. "But if you ain't your own self no more, why, Miss Cox be it. 'T seems to me's if I warn't my own self no more—'s if I'd got into some un else, or 't least hedn't got my own ears on m' own head.—Never saw or heerd Alice like this before!" he added, turning in gloomy bewilderment to the housemaid for a word of human sympathy.

The movement did not altogether please Alice, and she felt she must justify her behaviour.

"You see, John," she said, with dignity, keeping her back towards him, and pretending to dust the globe of a lamp, "there's things as no woman can help, and therefore as no man has no right to complain of them. It's not as if I'd gone an' done it, or changed myself, no more 'n if it 'ad took place in my cradle. What can I help it, if the world goes and changes itself? Am *I* to blame?—tell me that. It's not that I make no complaint, but I tell you it ain't me, it's circumstances is changed, things ain't the same as they was, and Miss is the properer term from you to me, John Jephson."

"Dang it if I know what you're a drivin' at, Alice!—Miss Cox!—and I beg yer perdon, miss, I'm sure,—Dang me if I do!"

"Don't swear, John Jephson—leastways before a lady. It's not proper."

"It seems to me, Miss Cox, as if the wind was a settin' from Bedlam, or maybe Colney Hatch," said John, who was considered a humourist among his comrades. "I wouldn't take no liberties with a lady, Miss Cox; but if I might be so bold as to arst the joke of the thing—"

"Joke, indeed!" cried Alice. "Do you call a dead uncle and ten thousand pounds a joke?"

"God bless me!" said John. "You don't mean it, Alice?"

"I do mean it, and that you'll find, John Jephson. I'm goin' to bid you good-bye tomorrer."

"Whoy, Alice!" exclaimed honest John, aghast.

"It's truth I tell ye," said Alice.

"And for how long?" gasped John, forefeeling illimitable misfortune.

"That depends," returned Alice, who did not care to lessen the effect of her communication by mentioning her promised return for a season. "—It ain't likely," she added, "as a heiress is goin' to act the nuss-maid much longer."

"But Alice," said John, "you don't mean to say—it's not in your mind now—it can't be, Alice—you're only jokin' with me—"

"Indeed, and I'm not!" interjected Alice, with a sniff.

"I don't mean that way, you know. What I mean is, you don't know as how this 'ere money—dang it all!—as how it's to be all over between you and me?—You *can't* mean that, Alice!" ended the poor fellow, with a choking in his throat.

It was very hard on him! He must either look as if he wanted to share her money, or else as if he were ready to give her up.

"Arst yourself, John Jephson," answered Alice, "whether it's likely a young lady of fortun' would be keepin' company with a young man as didn't know how to take off his hat to her in the park?"

Alice did not above half mean what she said: she wished mainly to enhance her own importance. At the same time she did mean it half, and that would have been enough for Jephson. He rose, grievously wounded.

"Good-bye, Alice," he said, taking the hand she did not refuse. "Ye're throwin' from ye what all yer money won't buy."

She gave a scornful little laugh, and John walked out of the kitchen.

At the door he turned with one lingering look; but in Alice there was no sign of softening. She turned scornfully away, and no doubt enjoyed her triumph to the full.

The next morning she went away.

CHAPTER IV

Mr. Greatorex had ceased to regard the advent of Christmas with much interest. Naturally gifted with a strong religious tendency, he had, since his first marriage, taken, not to denial, but to the side of objection, spending much energy in contempt for the foolish opinions of others, a self-indulgence which does less than little to further the growth of one's own spirit in truth and righteousness. The only person who stands excused—I do not say justified—in so doing, is the man who, having been taught the same opinions, has found them a legion of adversaries barring his way to truth. But having got rid of them for himself, it is, I suspect, worse than useless to attack them again, save as the ally of those who are fighting their way through the same ranks to the truth. Greatorex had been indulging his intellect at the expense of his heart. A man may have light in the brain and darkness in the heart. It were better to be an owl than a strong-eyed apteryx. He was on the path which naturally ends in blindness and unbelief. I fancy, if he had not been neglectful of his child, she would ere this time relighted his Christmas-candles for him; but now his second disappointment in marriage had so dulled his heart that he had begun to regard life as a stupid affair, in which the most enviable fool was the man who could still expect to realize an ideal. He had set out on a false track altogether, but had not yet discovered that there had been an immoral element at work in his mistake.

For what right had he to desire the fashioning of any woman after his ideas? Did not the angel of her eternal Ideal for ever behold the face of her Father in heaven? The best that can be said for him is, that, notwithstanding his own faults, which were, with all his cultivation and strength of character, yet more serious than hers, he was still kind to her; yes, I may say for him, notwithstanding even her silliness, which is a sickening fault, and one which no supremacy of beauty can overshadow, he still loved her a little. Hence the care he showed for her in respect of the coming sorrow was genuine. It did not all belong to his desire for a son to whom he might be a father indeed—after his own fancies, however. Letty, on her part, was as full of expectation as the girl who has been promised a doll that can shut and open its eyes, and cry when it is pinched; her carelessness of its safe arrival came of ignorance and not indifference.

It cannot but seem strange that such a man should have been so careless of the child he had. But from the first she had painfully reminded him of her mother, with whom in truth he had never quarrelled, but with whom he had not found life the less irksome on that account. Add to this that he had been growing fonder of business,—a fact which indicated, in a man of his endowment and development, an inclination downwards of the plane of his life. It was some time since he had given up reading poetry. History had almost followed: he now read little except politics, travels, and popular expositions of scientific progress.

That year Christmas Eve fell upon a Monday. The day before, Letty not feeling very well, her husband thought it better not to leave her, and gave up going to church. Phosy was utterly forgotten, but she dressed herself, and at the usual hour appeared with her prayer-book in her hand ready for church. When her father told her that he was not going, she looked so blank that he took pity upon her, and accompanied her to the church-door, promising to meet her as she came out. Phosy sighed from relief as she entered, for she had a vague idea that by going to church to pray for it she might move the Lord to chasten her. At least he would see her there, and might think of it. She had never had such an attention from her father before, never such dignity conferred upon her as to be allowed to appear in church alone, sitting in the pew by herself like a grown damsel. But I doubt if there was any pride in her stately step, or any vanity in the smile—no, not smile, but illuminated mist, the vapour of smiles, which haunted her sweet little solemn church-window of a face, as she walked up the aisle.

The preacher was one of whom she had never heard her father speak slighting word, in whom her unbound trust had never been shaken. Also he was one who believed with his own soul in the things that make Christmas precious. To him the birth of the wonderful baby hinted at hundreds of strange things in the economy of the planet. That a man could so thoroughly persuade himself that he believed the old fable, was matter of marvel to some of his friends who held blind Nature the eternal mother, and Night the everlasting grandmother of all things. But the child Phosy, in her dreams or out of them, in church or nursery, with her book or her doll, was never out of the region of wonders, and would have believed, or tried to believe, anything that did not involve a moral impossibility.

What the preacher said I need not even partially repeat; it is enough to mention a certain metamorphosed deposit from the stream of his elegance carried home in her mind by Phosy: from some of his sayings about the birth of Jesus into the world, into the family, into the individual human bosom, she had got it into her head that Christmas Day was not a birthday like that she had herself last year, but that, in some wonderful way, to her requiring no explanation, the baby Jesus was born every Christmas Day afresh. What became of him afterwards she did not know, and indeed she had never yet thought to ask how it was that he could come to every house in London as well as No. 1, Wimborne Square. Little of a home as others might think it, that house was yet to her the centre of all houses, and the wonder had not yet widened rippling beyond it: into that spot of the pool the eternal gift would fall.

Her father forgot the time over his book, but so entranced was her heart with the expectation of the promised visit, now so near—the day after to-morrow—that, if she had not altogether forgot to look for him as she stepped down the stair from the church door to the street, his absence caused her no uneasiness; and when, just as she reached it, he opened the house-door in tardy haste to redeem his promise, she looked up at him with a solemn, smileless repose, born of spiritual tension and speechless anticipation, upon her face, and walking past him without changing in the rhythm of her motion, marched stately up the stairs to the nursery. I believe the centre of her hope was that when the baby came she would beg him on her knees to ask the Lord to chasten her.

When dessert was over, her mother on the sofa in the drawing-room, and her father in an easy-chair, with a bottle of his favourite wine by his side, she crept out of the room and away again to the nursery. There she reached up to her little bookshelf, and, full of the sermon as spongy mists are full of the sunlight, took thence a volume of stories from the German, the re-reading of one of which, narrating the visit of the Christ-child, laden with gifts, to a certain household, and what he gave to each of them and all therein, she had, although sorely tempted, saved up until now and sat down with it by the fire, the only light she had. When the housemaid, suddenly remembering she must put her to bed, and at the same time discovering it was a whole hour past her usual time, hurried to the nursery, she found her fast asleep in her little arm-chair, her book on her lap, and the fire self-consumed into a dark cave with a sombre glow in its deepest hollows. Dreams had doubtless come to strengthen the impressions of sermon and *märchen*, for as she slowly yielded to the hands of Polly putting her to bed, her lips, unconsciously moved of the slumbering but not sleeping spirit, more than once murmured the words *Lord loveth and chasteneth*. Right blessedly would I enter the dreams of such a child—revel in them, as a bee in the heavenly gulf of a cactus-flower.

CHAPTER V

On Christmas Eve the church bells were ringing through the murky air of London, whose streets lay flaring and steaming below. The brightest of their constellations were the butchers' shops, with their shows of prize beef; around them, the eddies of the human tides were most confused and knotted. But the toy-shops were brilliant also. To Phosy they would have been the treasure caves of the Christ-child—all mysteries, all with insides to them—boxes, and desks, and windmills, and dove-cots, and hens with chickens, and who could tell what all? In every one of those shops her eyes would have searched for the Christ-child, the giver of all their wealth. For to her he was everywhere that night—ubiquitous as the luminous mist that brooded all over London—of which, however, she saw nothing but the glow above the mews. John Jephson was out in the middle of all the show, drifting about in it: he saw nothing that had pleasure in it, his heart was so heavy. He never thought once of the Christ-child, or even the Christman, as the giver of anything. Birth is the one standing promise-hope for the race, but for poor John this Christmas held no promise. With all his humour, he was one of those people, generally dull and slow—God grant me and mine such dulness and such sloth—who having once loved, cannot cease. During the fortnight he had scarce had a moment's ease from the sting of Alice's treatment. The honest fellow's feelings were no study to himself; he knew nothing but the pleasure and the pain of them; but I believe it was not mainly for himself that he was sorry. Like Athelia, "the pity of it" haunted him: he had taken Alice for a downright girl, about whom there was and could be no mistake; and the first hot blast of prosperity had swept her away like a hectic leaf. What were all the shops dressed out in holly and mistletoe, what were all the rushing flaming gas-jets, what the fattest of prize-pigs to John, who could never more imagine a spare-rib on the table between Alice and him of a Sunday? His imagination ran on seeing her pass in her carriage, and drop him a nod of condescension as she swept noisily by him—trudging home weary from his work to his loveless fireside. *He* didn't want her money! Honestly, he would rather have her without than with money, for now he regarded it as an enemy, seeing what evil changes it could work. "There be some devil in is, sure!" he said to himself. True, he had never found any in his week's wages, but he did remember once finding the devil in a month's wages received in the lump.

As he was thus thinking with himself, a carriage came suddenly from a side street into the crowd, and while he stared at it, thinking Alice might be sitting inside it while he was tramping the pavement alone, she passed him on the other side on foot—was actually pushed against him: he looked round, and saw a young woman, carrying a small bag, disappearing in the crowd. "There's an air of Alice about *her*," said John to himself, seeing her back only. But of course it couldn't be Alice; for he must look in the carriages now! And what a fool he was: every young woman reminded him of the one he had lost! Perhaps if he were to call the next day—Polly was a good-natured creature—he might hear some news of her.

It had been a troubled fortnight with Mrs. Greatorex. She wished much that she could have talked to her husband more freely, but she had not learned to feel at home with him. Yet he had been kinder and more attentive than usual all the time, so much so that Letty thought with herself—if she gave him a boy, he would certainly return to his first devotion. She said *boy*, because anyone might see he cared little for Phosy. She had never discovered that he was disappointed in herself, but, since her disregard of his wishes had brought evil upon her, she had begun to suspect that he had some ground for being dissatisfied with her. She never dreamed of his kindness as the effort of a conscientious nature to make the best of what could not now be otherwise helped. Her own poverty of spirit and lack of worth achieved, she knew as little of as she did of the riches of Michael the archangel. One must have begun to gather wisdom before he can see his own folly.

That evening she was seated alone in the drawing-room, her husband having left her to smoke his cigar, when the butler entered and informed her that Alice had returned, but was behaving so oddly that they did not know what to do with her. Asking wherein her oddness consisted, and learning that it was mostly in silence and tears, she was not sorry to gather that some disappointment had befallen her, and felt considerable curiosity to know what it was. She therefore told him to send her upstairs.

Meantime Polly, the housemaid, seeing plainly enough from her return in the middle of her holiday, and from her utter dejection, that Alice's expectations had been frustrated, and cherishing no little resentment against her because of her *uppishment* on the first news of her good fortune, had been ungenerous enough to take her revenge in a way as stinging in effect as bitter in intention; for she loudly protested that no amount of such luck as she pretended to suppose in Alice's possession, would have induced *her* to behave herself so that a handsome, honest fellow like John Jephson should be driven to despise her, and take up with her betters. When her mistress's message came, Alice was only too glad to find refuge from the kitchen in the drawing-room.

The moment she entered, she fell on her knees at the foot of the couch on which her mistress lay, covered her face with her hands, and sobbed grievously.

Nor was the change more remarkable in her bearing than in her person. She was pale and worn, and had a hunted look—was in face a mere shadow of what she had been. For a time her mistress found it impossible to quiet her so as to draw from her her story: tears and sobs combined with repugnance to hold her silent.

"Oh, ma'am!" she burst at length, wringing her hands "how ever *can* I tell you? You will never speak to me again. Little did I think such a disgrace was waiting me!"

"It was no fault of your own if you were misinformed," said her mistress, "or that your uncle was not the rich man you fancied."

"Oh, ma'am, there was no mistake there! He was more than twice as rich as I fancied. If he had only died a beggar and left things as they was!"

"Then he didn't leave it to his nephews and nieces as they told you?—Well, there's no disgrace in that."

"Oh! but he did, ma'am: that was all right; no mistake there either, ma'am.—And to think o' me behavin' as I did—to you and master as was so good to me! Who'll ever take notice of me now, after what has come out—as I'm sure I no more dreamed on than the child unborn!"

An agonized burst of fresh weeping followed, and it was with prolonged difficulty, and by incessant questioning, that Mrs. Greatorex at length drew from her the following facts.

Before Alice and her brother could receive the legacy to which they laid claim, it was necessary to produce certain documents, the absence of which, as of any proof to take their place, led to the unavoidable publication of a fact previously known to a living few—namely, that the father and mother of Alice Hopwood had never been married, which fact deprived them of the smallest claim on the legacy, and fell like a millstone upon Alice and her pride. From the height of her miserable arrogance she fell prone—not merely hurled back into the lowly condition from which she had raised her head only to despise it with base unrighteousness, and to adopt and reassert the principles she had abhorred when they affected herself—not merely this, but, in her own judgment at least, no longer the respectable member of society she had hitherto been justified in supposing herself. The relation of her father and mother she felt overshadow her with a disgrace unfathomable—the more overwhelming that it cast her from the gates of the Paradise she had seemed on the point of entering: her fall she measured by the height of the social ambition she had cherished, and had seemed on the point of attaining. But it is not an evil that the devil's money, which this legacy had from the first proved to Alice, should turn to a hot cinder in the hand. Rarely had a more haughty spirit than hers gone before a fall, and rarely had the fall been more sudden or more abject. And the consciousness of the behaviour into which her false riches had seduced her, changed the whip of her chastisement into scorpions. Worst of all, she had insulted her lover as beneath her notice, and the next moment she had found herself too vile for his. Judging by herself, in the injustice of bitter humiliation as she imagined him scoffing with his mates at the base-born menial who would set up for a fine lady. But had she been more worthy of honest John, she would have understood him better. As it was, no really good fortune could had befallen her but such as now seemed to her the depth of evil fortune. Without humiliation to prepare the way for humility, she must have become capable of more and more baseness, until she lost all that makes life worth having.

When Mrs. Greatorex had given her what consolation she found handy, and at length dismissed her, the girl, unable to endure her own company, sought the nursery, where she caught Phosy in her arms and embraced her with fervour. Never in her life having been the object of any such display of feeling, Phosy was much astonished: when Alice had set her down and she had resumed her seat by the fireside, she went on staring for awhile—and then a strange sort of miming ensued.

It was Phosy's habit—one less rare with children than may be most imagined—to do what she could to enter into any state of mind whose shows were sufficiently marked for her observation. She sought to lay hold of the feeling that produced the expression: less than the reproduction if a similar condition in her own imaginative sensorium, subject to her leisurely examination, would in no case satisfy the little metaphysician. But what was indeed very odd was the means she took of arriving at the sympathetic knowledge she desired. As if she had been the most earnest student of dramatic expression through the facial muscles, she would sit watching the countenance of the object of her solicitude, all the time with full consciousness, fashioning her own as nearly as she could into the lines and forms of the other: in proportion as she succeeded, the small psychologist imagined she felt in herself the condition that produced the phenomenon she observed—as if the shape of her face cast inward its shadow upon her mind, and so revealed to it, through the two faces, what was moving and shaping in the mind of the other.

In the present instance, having at length, after modelling and remodelling her face like that of a gutta-percha doll for some time, composed it finally into the best correspondence she could effect, she sat brooding for a while, with Alice's expression as it were frozen upon it. Gradually the forms assumed and melted away, and allowed her still, solemn face to look out from behind them. The moment this evanishment was complete, she rose and went to Alice, where she sat staring into the fire, unconscious of the scrutiny she had been undergoing, and looking up in her face, took her thumb out of her mouth, and said,

"Is the Lord chastening Alice? I wish he would chasten Phosy."

Her face was as calm as that of the Sphinx; there was no mist in the depth of her gray eyes, not a cloud on the wide heaven of her forehead.

Was the child crazed? What could the atom mean, with her big eyes looking right into her: it was indeed strange if the less should comprehend the greater! She was not yet capable of recognising the word of the Lord in the mouth of babes and sucklings. But there was a something in Phosy's face besides it calmness and unintelligibility. What it was Alice could never have told—yet it did her good. She lifted the child on her lap. There she soon fell asleep. Alice undressed her, laid her in her crib, and went to bed herself.

But, weary as she was, she had to rise again before she got to sleep. Her mistress was again taken ill. Doctor and nurse were sent for in hot haste; hansom cabs came and went throughout the night, like noisy moths to the one lighted house in the street; there were soft steps within, and doors were gently opened and shut. The waters of Mara had risen and filled the house.

Towards morning they were ebbing slowly away. Letty did not know that her husband was watching by her bedside. The street was quiet now. So was the house. Most of its people had been up throughout the night, but now they had all gone to bed except the strange nurse and Mr. Greatorex.

It was the morning of Christmas Day, and little Phosy knew it in every cranny of her soul. She was not of those who had been up all night, and now she was awake, early and wide, and the moment she awoke she was speculating. He was coming to-day—*how* would he come? Where should she find the baby Jesus? And when would he come? In the morning, or the afternoon, or in the evening? Could such a grief be in store for her as that he would not appear before night, when she would be again in bed? But she would not sleep till all hope was gone. Would everybody be gathered to meet him, or would he show himself to one after another, each alone? Then her turn would be last, and oh, if he would not come to the nursery! But perhaps he would not appear to her at all!—for was she not one whom the Lord did not care to chasten?

Expectation grew and wrought in her until she could lie in bed no longer. Alice was fast asleep. It must be early, but whether it was yet light or not she could not tell for the curtains. Anyhow she would get up and dress, and then she would be ready for Jesus whenever he should come. True, she was not able to dress herself very well, but he would know, and would not mind. She made all the haste she could, consistently with taking pains, and was soon attired after a fashion.

She crept out of the room and down the stair. The house was very still. What if Jesus should come and find nobody awake? Would he go again and give them no presents? She couldn't expect any herself—but might he not let her take theirs for the rest? Perhaps she ought to wake them all, but she dared not without being sure.

On the last landing above the first floor, she saw, by the low gaslight at the end of the corridor, an unknown figure pass the foot of the stair: could she have anything to do with the marvel of the day? The woman looked up, and Phosy dropped the question. Yet she might be a charwoman, whose assistance the expected advent rendered necessary. When she reached the bottom of the stair she saw her disappearing in her step-mother's room. That she did not like. It was the one room in which she could not go. But, as the house was so still, she would search everywhere else, but if she did not find him, would then sit down in the hall and wait for him.

The room next the foot of the stairs, and opposite her step-mother's was the spare room, with which she associated ideas of state and grandeur: where better could she begin than in the guest-chamber? There!—Could it be? Yes!—Through the chink of the scarce-closed door she saw light. Either he was already there or there they were expecting him. From that moment she felt as lifted out of the body. Far exalted above all dread, she peeped modestly in, and then entered. Beyond the foot of the bed, a candle stood on a little low table, but nobody was to be seen. There was a stool near the table: she would sit on it by the candle, and wait for him. But ere she reached it, she caught sight of something upon the bed that drew her thither. She stood entranced.—*Could* it be?—It *might* be. Perhaps he had left it there while he went into her mamma's room with something for her,—The loveliest of dolls ever imagined! She drew nearer. The light was low, and the shadows were many: she could not be sure it was. But when she had gone close up to it, she concluded with certainty that it was in very truth a doll—perhaps intended for her—but beyond doubt the most exquisite of dolls. She dragged a chair to the bed, got up, pushed her little arms softly under it, and drawing it gently to her, slid down with it. When she felt her feet firm on the floor, filled with the solemn composure of holy awe she carried the gift of the child Jesus to the candle, that she might the better admire its beauty and know its preciousness. But the light had no sooner fallen upon it than a strange undefinable doubt awoke within her. Whatever it was, it was the very essence of loveliness—the tiny darling with its alabaster face, and its delicately modelled hands and fingers! A long night-gown covered the rest.—Was it possible?—Could it be?—Yes, indeed! it must be—it could be nothing else than a *real* baby! What a goose she had been! Of course it was baby Jesus himself!—for was not this his very own Christmas Day on which he was always born?—If she had felt awe of his gift before, what a grandeur of adoring love, what a divine dignity possessed her, holding in her arms the very child himself! One shudder of bliss passed through her, and in an agony of possession she clasped the baby to her great heart—then at once became still with the satisfaction of eternity, with the peace of God. She sat down on the stool, near the little table, with her back to the candle, that its rays should not fall on the eyes of the sleeping Jesus and wake him: there she sat, lost in the very majesty of bliss, at once the mother and the slave of the Lord Jesus.

She sat for a time still as marble waiting for marble to awake, heedful as tenderest woman not to rouse him before his time, though her heart was swelling with the eager petition that he would ask his Father to be as good as chasten her. And as she sat, she began, after her wont, to model her face to the likeness of his, that she might understand his stillness—the absolute peace that dwelt on his countenance. But as she did so, again a sudden doubt invaded her: Jesus lay so very still—never moved, never opened his pale eye-lids! And now set thinking, she noted that he did not breathe. She had seen babies asleep, and their breath came and went—their little bosoms heaved up and down, and sometimes they would smile, and sometimes they would moan and sigh. But Jesus did none of these things: was it not strange? And then he was cold—oh, so cold!

A blue silk coverlid lay on the bed: she half rose and dragged it off, and contrived to wind it around herself and the baby. Sad at heart, very sad, but undismayed, she sat and watched him on her lap.

CHAPTER VI

Meantime the morning of Christmas Day grew. The light came and filled the house. The sleepers slept late, but at length they stirred. Alice awoke last—from a troubled sleep, in which the events of the night mingled with her own lost condition and destiny. After all Polly had been kind, she thought, and got Sophy up without disturbing her.

She had been but a few minutes down, when a strange and appalling rumour made itself—I cannot say audible, but—somehow known through the house, and everyone hurried up in horrible dismay.

The nurse had gone into the spare room and missed the little dead thing she had laid there. The bed was between her and Phosy, and she never saw her. The doctor had been sharp with her about something the night before: she now took her revenge in suspicion of him, and after a hasty and fruitless visit of inquiry to the kitchen, hurried to Mr. Greatorex.

The servants crowded to the spare room, and when their master, incredulous indeed, yet shocked at the tidings brought him, hastened to the spot, he found them all in the room, gathered at the foot of the bed. A little sunlight filtered through the red window-curtains, and gave a strange pallid expression to the flame of the candle, which had now burned very low. At first he saw nothing but the group of servants, silent, motionless, with heads leaning forward, intently gazing: he had come just in time: another moment and they would have ruined the lovely sight. He stepped forward, and saw Phosy, half shrouded in blue, the candle behind illuminating the hair she had found too rebellious to the brush, and making of it a faint aureole about her head and white face, whence cold and sorrow had driven all the flush, rendering it colourless as that upon her arm which had never seen the light. She had pored on the little face until she knew death, and now she sat a speechless mother of sorrow, bending in the dim light of the tomb over the body of her holy infant.

How it was I cannot tell, but the moment her father saw her she looked up, and the spell of her dumbness broke.

"Jesus is dead," she said, slowly and sadly, but with perfect calmness. "He is dead," she repeated. "He came too early, and there was no one up to take care of him, and he's dead—dead—dead!"

But as she spoke the last words, the frozen lump of agony gave way; the well of her heart suddenly filled, swelled, overflowed; the last word was half sob, half shriek of utter despair and loss.

Alice darted forward and took the dead baby tenderly from her. The same moment her father raised the little mother and clasped her to his bosom. Her arms went round his neck, her head sank on his shoulder, and sobbing in grievous misery, yet already a little comforted, he bore her from the room.

"No, no, Phosy!" they heard him say, "Jesus is not dead, thank God. It is only your little brother that hadn't life enough, and is gone back to God for more."

Weeping, the women went down the stairs. Alice's tears were still flowing, when John Jephson entered. Her own troubles forgotten in the emotion of the scene she had just witnessed, she ran to his arms and wept on his bosom.

John stood as one astonished.

"O Lord! this *is* a Christmas!" he sighed at last.

"Oh John!" cried Alice, and tore herself from his embrace, "I forgot! You'll never speak to me again, John! Don't do it, John."

And with the words she gave a stifled cry, and fell a-weeping again, behind her shielding two hands.

"Why, Alice!—you ain't married, are you?" gasped John, to whom that was the only possible evil.

"No, John, and never shall be: a respectable man like you would never think of looking twice at a poor girl like me!"

"Let's have one more look anyhow," said John, drawing her hands from her face. "Tell me what's the matter, and if there's anything can be done to right you, I'll work day and night to do it, Alice."

"There's nothing *can* be done, John," replied Alice, and would again have floated out on the ocean of her misery, but in spite of wind and tide, that is, sobs and tears, she held on by the shore at his entreaty, and told her tale, not even omitting the fact that when she went to the eldest of the cousins, inheriting through the misfortune of her and her brother so much more than their expected share, and "demeaned herself" to beg a little help for her brother, who was dying of consumption, he had all but ordered her out of the house, swearing he had nothing to do with her or her brother, and saying she ought to be ashamed to show her face.

"And that when we used to make mud pies together!" concluded Alice with indignation. "There, John! you have it all," she added. "——And now?"

With the word she gave a deep, humbly questioning look into his honest eyes.

"Is that all, Alice?" he asked.

"Yes, John; ain't it enough?" she returned.

"More'n enough," answered John. "I swear to you, Alice, you're worth to me ten times what you would ha' been, even if you ha' had me, with ten thousand pounds in your ridicule. Why, my woman, I never saw you look one 'alf so 'an'some as you do now!"

"But the disgrace of it, John!" said Alice, hanging her head, and so hiding the pleasure that would dawn through all the mist of her misery.

"Let your father and mother settle that betwixt 'em, Alice. 'Taint none o' my business. Please God, we'll do different.—When shall it be, my girl?"

"When you like, John," answered Alice, without raising her head, thoughtfully.

When she had withdrawn herself from the too rigorous embrace with which he received her consent, she remarked—

"I do believe, John, money ain't a good thing! Sure as I live, with the very wind o' that money, the devil entered into me. Didn't you hate me, John? Speak the truth now."

"No, Alice, I did cry a bit over you, though. You *was* possessed like."

"I *was* possessed. I do believe if that money hadn't been took from me, I'd never ha' had you, John. Ain't it awful to think on?"

"Well, no. O' course! How could ye?" said Jephson—with reluctance.

"Now, John, don't ye talk like that, for I won't stand it. Don't you go for to set me up again with excusin' of me. I'm a nasty conceited cat, I am—and all for nothing but mean pride."

"Mind ye, ye're mine now, Alice; an' what's mine's mine, an' I won't have it abused. I knows you twice the woman you was afore, and all the world couldn't gi' me such another Christmas-box—no, not as if it was all gold watches and roast beef."

When Mr. Greatorex returned to his wife's room, and thought to find her asleep as he had left her, he was dismayed to hear sounds of soft weeping from the bed. Some tone or stray word, never intended to reach her ear, had been enough to reveal the truth concerning her baby.

"Hush! hush!" he said, with more love in his heart than had moved there for many months, and therefore more in his tone than she had heard for as many;—"if you cry you will be ill. Hush, my dear!"

In a moment ere he could prevent, she had flung her arms around his neck as he stooped over her.

"Husband! husband!" she cried, "is it my fault?"

"You behaved perfectly," he returned. "No woman could have been braver."

"Ah, but I wouldn't stay at home when you wanted me."

"Never mind that now, my child," he said.

At the word she pulled his face down to hers.

"I have *you*, and I don't care," he added.

"Do you care to have me?" she said, with a sob that ended in a loud cry. "Oh! I don't deserve it. But I *will* be good after this. I promise you I will."

"Then you must begin now, my darling. You must lie perfectly still, and not cry a bit, or you will go after the baby, and I shall be left alone."

She looked up at him with such a light in her face as he had never dreamed of there before. He had never seen her so lovely. Then she withdrew her arms, repressed her tears, smiled, and turned her face away. He put her hands under the clothes, and in a minute or two she was again fast asleep.

CHAPTER VII

That day, when Phosy and her father had sat down to their Christmas dinner, he rose again, and taking her up as she sat, chair and all, set her down close to him, on the other side of the corner of the table. It was the first of a new covenant between them. The father's eyes having suddenly opened to her character and preciousness, as well as to his own neglected duty in regard to her, it was as if a well of life had burst forth at his feet. And every day, as he looked in her face and talked to her, it was with more and more respect for what he found in her, with growing tenderness for her predilections, and reverence for the divine idea enclosed in her ignorance, for her childish wisdom, and her calm seeking—until at length he would have been horrified at the thought of training her up in *his* way: had she not a way of her own to go—following—not the dead Jesus, but Him who liveth for evermore? In the endeavour to help her, he had to find his own position towards the truth; and the results were weighty.—Nor did the child's influence work forward merely. In his intercourse with her he was so often reminded of his first wife, and that with the gloss or comment of a childish reproduction, that his memories of her at length grew a little tender, and through the child he began to understand the nature and worth of the mother. In her child she had given him what she could not be herself. Unable to keep up with him, she had handed him her baby, and dropped on the path.

Nor was little Sophy his only comfort. Through their common loss and her husband's tenderness, Letty began to grow a woman. And her growth was the more rapid that, himself taught through Phosy, her husband no longer desired to make her adopt his tastes, and judge with his experiences, but, as became the elder and the tried, entered into her tastes and experiences—became, as it were, a child again with her, that, through the thing she was, he might help the thing she had to be.

As soon as she was able to bear it, he told her the story of the dead Jesus, and with the tale came to her heart love for Phosy. She had lost a son for a season, but she had gained a daughter for ever.

Such were the gifts the Christ-child brought to one household that

Christmas. And the days of the mourning of that household were ended.

Poems

The Mother Mary: I

Mary to thy heart was given
For infant hand to hold,
And clasp thus, an eternal heaven,
The great earth in its fold.

He seized the world with tender might
By making thee his own;
Thee, lowly queen, whose heavenly height
Was to thyself unknown.

He came, all helpless, to thy power,
For warmth, and love, and birth;
In thy embraces, every hour,
He grew into the earth.

Thine was the grief, O mother high,
Which all thy sisters share
Who keep the gate betwixt the sky
And in our lower air;

But unshared sorrows, gathering slow,
Will rise within the heart,
Strange thoughts which like a sword will go
Thorough thy inward part.

For, if a woman bore a son
That was of angel brood,
Who lifted wings ere day was done,
And soared from where she stood,

Wild grief would rave on love's high throne;
She, sitting in the door,
All day would cry: "He was my own,
And now is mine no more!"

So thou, O Mary, years on years,
From child-birth to the cross,

Wast filled with yearnings, filled with fears,
Keen sense of love and loss.

His childish thoughts outsoared thy reach;
His godlike tenderness
Would sometimes seem, in human speech,
To thee than human less.

Strange pangs await thee, mother mild,
A sorer travail-pain;
Then will the spirit of thy child
Be born in thee again.

There then thou wilt forebode and dread;
Loss will be still thy fear—
Till he be gone, and, in his stead,
His very self appear.

For, when thy son hath reached his goal,
And vanished from the earth,
Soon wilt thou find him in thy soul,
A second, holier birth.

A Christmas Carol for 1862

The Year of the Trouble in Lancashire

The skies are pale, the trees are stiff,
    The earth is dull and old;
The frost is glittering as if
    The very sun were cold.
And hunger fell is joined with frost,
    To make men thin and wan:
Come, Babe, from heaven, or we are lost;
    Be born, O child of man.

The children cry, the women shake,
    The strong men stare about;
They sleep when they should be awake,
    They wake ere night is out.
For they have lost their heritage—
    No sweat is on their brow:
Come, babe, and bring them work and wage;
    Be born, and save us now.

Across the sea, beyond our sight,
    Roars on the fierce debate;
The men go down in bloody fight,
    The women weep and hate;
And in the right be which they may,
    Surely the strife is long!
Come, son of man, thy righteous way,
    And right will have no wrong.

Good men speak lies against thine own—
    Tongue quick, and hearing slow;
They will not let thee walk alone,
    And think to serve thee so:
If they the children's freedom saw
    In thee, the child's king,
They would be still with holy awe,
    Or only speak to sing.

Some neither lie nor starve nor fight,
    Nor yet the poor deny;
But in their hearts all is not right,—
    They often sit and sigh.
We need thee every day and hour,
    In sunshine and in snow:
Child-king, we pray with all our power—
    Be born, and save us so.

We are but men and women, Lord;
    Thou art a gracious child!
O fill our hearts, and heap our board,
    Pray thee—the winter's wild!
The sky is sad, the trees are bare,
    Hunger and hate about:
Come, child, and ill deeds and ill fare
    Will soon be driven out.

A Christmas Carol

Babe Jesus lay in Mary's lap,
   The sun shone in his hair;
And this is how she saw, mayhap,
   The crown already there.

For she sang: "Sleep on, my little king;
   Bad Herod dares not come;
Before thee sleeping, holy thing,
   The wild winds would be dumb."

"I kiss thy hands, I kiss thy feet,
   My child, so long desired;
Thy hands will never be soiled, my sweet;
   Thy feet will never be tired."

"For thou art the king of men, my son;
   Thy crown I see it plain!
And men shall worship thee, every one,
   And cry, Glory! Amen!"

Babe Jesus he opened his eyes wide—
   At Mary looked her lord.
Mother Mary stinted her song and sighed;
   Babe Jesus said never a word.

The Sleepless Jesus

'Tis time to sleep, my little boy:
    Why gaze thy bright eyes so?
At night our children, for new joy
    Home to thy father go,
But thou art wakeful! Sleep my child;
    The moon and stars are gone;
The wind is up and raving wild,
    But thou art smiling on!

My child, thou hast immortal eyes
    That see by their own light;
They see the children's blood—it lies
    Red-glowing through the night!
Thou hast an ever-open ear
    For sob to cry or moan:
Thou seemest not to see or hear,
    Thou only smilest on!

When first thou camest to the earth,
    All sounds of strife were still;
A silence lay about thy birth,
    And thou didst sleep thy fill:
Thou wakest now—why weep'st thou not?
    Thy earth is woe-begone;
Both babes and mothers wail their lot,
    But still thou smilest on!

I read thy face like holy book;
    No hurt is pictured there;
Deep in thine eyes I see the look
    Of one who answers prayer.
Beyond pale grief and wild uproars,
    Thou seest God's will well done;
Low prayers, through chambers' closed doors,
    Thou hear'st—and smilest on.

Men say: "I will arise and go;"
 God says: "I will go meet:"
Thou seest them gather, weeping low,
 About the Father's feet;
And each for each begin to bear,
 And standing lonely none:
Answered, O eyes, ye see all prayer!
 Smile, Son of God, smile on.

Christmas, 1873

Christmas-Days are still in store:—
    Will they change—steal faded hither?
Or come fresh as heretofore,
    Summering all our winter weather?

Surely they will keep their bloom
    All the countless pacing ages:
In the country whence they come
    Children only are the sages!

Hither, every hour and year,
    Children come to cure our oldness—
Oft, alas, to gather sear
    Unbelief, and earthy boldness!

Men they grow and women cold,
    Selfish, passionate, and plaining!
Ever faster they grow old:—
    On the world, ah, eld is gaining!

Child, whose childhood ne'er departs!
    Jesus, with the perfect father!
Drive the age from parents' hearts;
    To thy heart the children gather.

Send thy birth into our souls,
    With its grand and tender story.
Hark! the gracious thunder rolls!—
    News to men! to God old glory!

Christmas, 1884

Though in my heart no Christmas glee,
   Though my song-bird be dumb,
Jesus, it is enough for me
   That thou art come.

What though the loved be scattered far,
   Few at the board appear,
In thee, O Lord, they gathered are,
   And thou art here.

And if our hearts be low with lack,
   They are not therefore numb;
Not always will thy day come back—
   Thyself will come!

An Old Story

In the ancient house of ages,
   See, they cannot rest!
With a hope, which awe assuages,
   Tremble all the blest.
For the son and heir eternal,
   To be son yet more,
Leaves his stately chair supernal
   For the earth's low floor;

Leaves the room so high and old,
   Leaves the all-world hearth,
Seeks the out-air, frosty-cold,
   Of the twilight earth—
To be throned in newer glory
   In a mother's lap,
Gather up our broken story,
   And right every hap.

II.

There Earth's foster-baby lies,
   Sleep-dimmed all his graces,
'Neath four stars of parents' eyes,
   And two heavens of faces!
See! the cow and ass, dumb-staring,
   Feel the skirts of good
Fold them in dull-blessed sharing
   Of infinitude.

Make a little room betwixt you,
   Pray you, Ass and Cow!
Sure we shall, if I kneel next you,
   Know each other now!
To the pit-fallen comes salvation—
   Love is never loath!

Here we are, thy whole creation,
    Waiting, Lord, thy growth!

III.

On the slopes of Bethlehem,
    Round their resting sheep,
Shepherds sat, and went and came,
    Guarding holy sleep;
But the silent, high dome-spaces,
    Airy galleries,
Thronged they were with watching faces,
    Thronged with open eyes.

Far across the desert floor,
    Come, slow-drawing nigher,
Sages deep in starry lore,
    Priests of burning Fire.
In the sky they read his story,
    And, through starlight cool,
They come riding to the Glory,
    To the Wonderful.

IV.

Babe and mother, coming Mage,
    Shepherd, ass, and cow!
Angels watching the new age,
    Time's intensest Now!
Heaven down-brooding, Earth upstraining,
    Far ends closing in!
Sure the eternal tide is gaining
    On the strand of sin!

See! but see! Heaven's chapel-master
    Sighs with lifted hand;
Winds divine blow fast and faster,
    Swelling bosoms grand.
Hark the torrent-joy let slip!
    Hark the great throats ring!

Glory! Peace! Good-fellowship!
  And a Child for king!

A Song for Christmas

Hark, in the steeple the dull bell swinging
  Over the furrows ill ploughed by Death!
Hark the bird-babble, the loud lark singing!
  Hark, from the sky, what the prophet saith!

Hark, in the pines, the free Wind, complaining—
  Moaning, and murmuring, "Life is bare!"
Hark, in the organ, the caught Wind, outstraining,
  Jubilant rise in a soaring prayer!

Toll for the burying, sexton tolling!
  Sing for the second birth, angel Lark!
Moan, ye poor Pines, with the Past condoling!
  Burst out, brave Organ, and kill the Dark!

II.

Sit on the ground, and immure thy sorrow;
  I will give freedom to mine in song!
Haunt thou the tomb, and deny the morrow;
  I will go watch in the dawning long!

For I shall see them, and know their faces—
  Tenderer, sweeter, and shining more;
Clasp the old self in the new embraces;
  Gaze through their eyes' wide open door.

Loved ones, I come to see you: see my sadness;
  I am ashamed—but you pardon wrong!
Smile the old smile, and my soul's new gladness
  Straight will arise in sorrow and song!

Christmas Song of the Old Children

Well for youth to seek the strong,
    Beautiful, and brave!
We, the old, who walk along
    Gently to the grave,
Only pay our court to thee,
Child of all Eternity!

We are old who once were young,
    And we grow more old;
Songs we are that have been sung,
    Tales that have been told;
Yellow leaves, wind-blown to thee,
Childhood of Eternity!

If we come too sudden near,
    Lo, Earth's infant cries,
For our faces wan and drear
    Have such withered eyes!
Thou, Heaven's child, turn'st not away
From the wrinkled ones who pray!

Smile upon us with thy mouth
    And thine eyes of grace;
On our cold north breathe thy south.
    Thaw the frozen face:
Childhood all from thee doth flow—
Melt to song our age's snow.

Gray-haired children come in crowds,
    Thee their Hope, to greet:
Is it swaddling clothes or shrouds
    Hampering so our feet?
Eldest child, the shadows gloom:
Take the aged children home.

We have had enough of play,
    And the wood grows drear;

Many who at break of day
   Companied us here—
They have vanished out of sight,
Gone and met the coming light!

Fair is this out-world of thine,
   But its nights are cold;
And the sun that makes it fine
   Makes us soon so old!
Long its shadows grow and dim—
Father, take us back with him!

Christmas Meditation

He who by a mother's love
    Made the wandering world his own,
Every year comes from above,
    Comes the parted to atone,
    Binding Earth to the Father's throne.

Nay, thou comest every day!
    No, thou never didst depart!
Never hour has been away!
    Always with us, Lord, thou art,
    Binding, binding heart to heart!

Christmas Prayer

Cold my heart, and poor, and low,
    Like thy stable in the rock;
Do not let it orphan go,
    It is of the parent stock!
Come thou in, and it will grow
    High and wide, a fane divine;
Like the ruby it will glow,
    Like the diamond shine!

Song of the Innocents

Merry, merry we well may be,
For Jesus Christ is come down to see:
Long before, at top of the stair,
He set our angels a waiting there,
Waiting hither and thither to fly,
Tending the children of the sky,
Lest they dash little feet against big stones,
And tumble down and break little bones;
For the path is rough, and we must not roam;
We have learned to walk, and must follow him home!

Christmas Day and Every Day

Star high,
Baby low:
'Twixt the two
Wise men go;
Find the baby,
Grasp the star—
Heirs of all things
Near and far!

A Father to a Mother

When God's own child came down to earth,
  High heaven was very glad;
The angels sang for holy mirth;
  Not God himself was sad!

Shall we, when ours goes homeward, fret?
  Come, Hope, and wait on Sorrow!
The little one will not forget;
  It's only till to-morrow!

Master and Boy

"Who is this little one lying,"
    Said Time, "at my garden-gate,
Moaning and sobbing and crying,
    Out in the cold so late?"

"They lurked until we came near,
    Master and I," the child said,
"Then caught me, with 'Welcome, New-year!
    Happy Year! Golden-head!'

"See Christmas-day, my Master,
    On the meadow a mile away!
Father Time, make me run faster!
    I'm the Shadow of Christmas-day!"

"Run, my child; still he's in sight!
    Only look well to his track;
Little Shadow, run like the light,
    He misses you at his back!"

Old Time sat down in the sun
    On a grave-stone—his legs were numb:
"When the boy to his master has run,"
    He said, "Heaven's New Year is come!"

The Mistletoe

Kiss me: there now, little Neddy,
Do you see her staring steady?
There again you have a chance of her!
Didn't you catch the pretty glance of her?
See her nest! On any planet
Never was a sweeter than it!
Never nest was such as this is:
'Tis the nest of all the kisses,
With the mother kiss-bird sitting
All through Christmas, never flitting,
Kisses, kisses, kisses hatching,
Sweetest birdies, for the catching!
Oh, the precious little brood
Always in a loving mood!—
There's one under Mammy's hood!

There, that's one I caught this minute,
Musical as any linnet!
Where it is, your big eyes question,
With of doubt a wee suggestion?
There it is—upon mouth merry!
There it is—upon cheek cherry!
There's another on chin-chinnie!
Now it's off, and lights on Minnie!
There's another on nose-nosey!
There's another on lip-rosy!
And the kissy-bird is hatching
Hundreds more for only catching.

Why the mistletoe she chooses,
And the Christmas-tree refuses?
There's a puzzle for your mother?
I'll present you with another!
Tell me why, you question-asker,
Cruel, heartless mother-tasker—
Why, of all the trees before her,
Gathered round, or spreading o'er her,

Jenny Wren should choose the apple
For her nursery and chapel!
Or Jack Daw build in the steeple
High above the praying people!
Tell me why the limping plover
O'er moist meadow likes to hover;
Why the partridge with such trouble
Builds her nest where soon the stubble
Will betray her hop-thumb-cheepers
To the eyes of all the reapers!—
Tell me, Charley; tell me, Janey;
Answer all, or answer any,
And I'll tell you, with much pleasure,
Why this little bird of treasure
Nestles only in the mistletoe,
Never, never goes the thistle to.

   Not an answer? Tell without it?
Yes—all that I know about it:—
Mistletoe, then, cannot flourish,
Cannot find the food to nourish
But on other plant when planted—
And for kissing two are wanted.
That is why the kissy-birdie
Looks about for oak-tree sturdy
And the plant that grows upon it
Like a wax-flower on a bonnet.

   But, my blessed little mannie,
All the birdies are not cannie
That the kissy-birdie hatches!
Some are worthless little patches,
Which indeed if they don't smutch you,
'Tis they're dead before they touch you!
While for kisses vain and greedy,
Kisses flattering, kisses needy,
They are birds that never waddled
Out of eggs that only addled!
Some there are leave spots behind them,
On your cheeks for years you'd find them:

Little ones, I do beseech you,
Never let such birdies reach you.

It depends what net you venture
What the sort of bird will enter!
I will tell you in a minute
What net takes kiss—lark or linnet—
Any bird indeed worth hatching
And just therefore worth the catching:
The one net that never misses
Catching at least some true kisses,
Is the heart that, loving truly,
Always loves the old love newly;
But to spread out would undo it—
Let the birdies fly into it.

King Cole

King Cole he reigned in Aureoland,
But sceptre was seldom in his hand

Far oftener was there his golden cup—
He ate too much, but he drank all up!

To be called a king and to be a king,
That is one thing and another thing!

So his majesty's head began to shake,
And his hands and feet to swell and ache,

The doctors were called, but they dared not say
Your majesty drinks too much Tokay;

So out of the king's heart died all mirth,
And he thought there was nothing good on earth.

Then up rose the fool, whose every word
Was three parts wise and one part absurd.

Nuncle, he said, never mind the gout;
I will make you laugh till you laugh it out.

King Cole pushed away his full gold plate:
The jester he opened the palace gate,

Brought in a cold man, with hunger grim,
And on the dais-edge seated him;

Then caught up the king's own golden plate,
And set it beside him: oh, how he ate!

And the king took note, with a pleased surprise,
That he ate with his mouth and his cheeks and his eyes,

With his arms and his legs and his body whole,
And laughed aloud with his heart and soul.

Then from his lordly chair he got up,
And carried the man his own gold cup;

The goblet was deep and wide and full,
The poor man ate like a cow at a pool.

Said the king to the jester—I call it well done
To drink with two mouths instead of one!

Said the king to himself, as he took his seat,
It is quite as good to feed as to eat!

It is better, I began to think,
To give to the thirsty than to drink!

And now I have thought of it, said the king,
There might be more of this kind of thing!

The fool heard. The king had not long to wait:
The fool cried aloud at the palace-gate;

The ragged and wretched, the hungry and thin,
Loose in their clothes and tight in their skin,

Gathered in shoals till they filled the hall,
And the king and the fool they fed them all;

And as with good things their plates they piled
The king grew merry as a little child.

On the morrow, early, he went abroad
And sought poor folk in their own abode—

Sought them till evening foggy and dim,
Did not wait till they came to him;

And every day after did what he could,
Gave them work and gave them food.

Thus he made war on the wintry weather,
And his health and the spring came back together.

But, lo, a change had passed on the king,
Like the change of the world in that same spring!

His face had grown noble and good to see,
And the crown sat well on his majesty.

Now he ate enough, and ate no more,
He drank about half what he drank before,

He reigned a real king of Aureoland,
He reigned with his head and his heart and his hand.

All this through the fool did come to pass.
And every Christmas-eve that was,

The palace-gates stood open wide
And the poor came in from every side,

And the king rose up and served them duly,
And his people loved him very truly.

The Christmas Child

"Little one, who straight has come
Down the heavenly stair,
Tell us all about your home,
And the father there."

"He is such a one as I,
Like as like can be.
Do his will, and, by and by,
Home and him you'll see."

A Christmas Prayer

Loving looks the large-eyed cow,
Loving stares the long-eared ass
At Heaven's glory in the grass!
Child, with added human birth
Come to bring the child of earth
Glad repentance, tearful mirth,
And a seat beside the hearth
At the Father's knee—
Make us peaceful as thy cow;
Make us patient as thine ass;
Make us quiet as thou art now;
Make us strong as thou wilt be.
Make us always know and see
We are his as well as thou.

Christmas-Day, 1878

I think I might be weary of this day
That comes inevitably every year,
The same when I was young and strong and gay,
The same when I am old and growing sere—
I should grow weary of it every year
But that thou comest to me every day.

I shall grow weary if thou every day
But come to me, Lord of eternal life;
I shall grow weary thus to watch and pray,
For ever out of labour into strife;
Take everlasting house with me, my life,
And I shall be new-born this Christmas-day.

Thou art the Eternal Son, and born no day,
But ever he the Father, thou the Son;
I am his child, but ever born alway—
How long, O Lord, how long till it be done?
Be thou from endless years to years the Son—
And I thy brother, new-born every day.

Christmas Day, 1850

Beautiful stories wed with lovely days
   Like words and music:—what shall be the tale
   Of love and nobleness that might avail
To express in action what his sweetness says—

The sweetness of a day of airs and rays
   That are strange glories on the winter pale?
   Alas, O beauty, all my fancies fail!
I cannot tell a story in thy praise!

Thou hast, thou hast one—set, and sure to chime
   With thee, as with the days of "winter wild,"
     For Joy like Sorrow loves his blessed feet
Who shone from Heaven on Earth this Christmas-time
   A Brother and a Saviour, Mary's child!—
     And so, fair day, thou *hast* thy story sweet.

That Holy Thing

They all were looking for a king
   To slay their foes, and lift them high:
Thou cam'st a little baby thing
   That made a woman cry.

O son of man, to right my lot
   Nought but thy presence can avail;
Yet on the road thy wheels are not,
   Nor on the sea thy sail!

My fancied ways why shouldst thou heed?
   Thou com'st down thine own secret stair:
Com'st down to answer all my need,
   Yea, every bygone prayer!

Christmas, 1880

Great-hearted child, thy very being *The Son*
  Who know'st the hearts of all us prodigals,—
For who is prodigal but he who has gone
  Far from the true to heart it with the false?—
  Who, who but thou, that, from the animals',
    Know'st all the hearts, up to the Father's own,
    Can tell what it would be to be alone!

Alone! No father!—At the very thought
  Thou, the eternal light, was once aghast;
A death in death for thee it almost wrought!
  But thou didst haste, about to breathe thy last,
  And call'dst out *Father* ere thy spirit passed,
    Exhausted in fulfilling not any vow,
    But doing his will who greater is than thou.

That we might know him, thou didst come and live;
  That we might find him, thou didst come and die;
The son-heart, brother, thy son-being give—
  We too would love the father perfectly,
  And to his bosom go back with the cry,
    Father, into thy hands I give the heart
    Which left thee but to learn how great thou art!

There are but two in all the universe—
  The father and his children—not a third;
Nor, all the weary time, fell any curse!
  Not once dropped from its nest an unfledged bird
  But thou wast with it! Never sorrow stirred
    But a love-pull it was upon the chain
    That draws the children to the father again!

O Jesus Christ, babe, man, eternal son,
  Take pity! we are poor where thou art rich:
Our hearts are small; and yet there is not one
  In all thy father's noisy nursery which,
  Merry, or mourning in its narrow niche,

Needs not thy father's heart, this very now,
With all his being's being, even as thou!

From Heaven Above

after Martin Luther

From heaven above I come to you,
To bring a story good and new:
Of goodly news so much I bring,
I cannot help it, I must sing.

To you a child is born this morn,
A child of holy maiden born,
A little babe, so sweet and mild,
It is a joy to see the child.

'Tis little Jesus, whom we need
Us out of sadness all to lead:
He will himself our Saviour be,
And from all sinning set us free.

Here come the shepherds, whom we know;
Let all of us right gladsome go,
To see what God to us hath given—
A gift that makes a stable heaven.

Take heed, my heart! Be lowly. So
Thou seest him lie in manger low:
That is the baby sweet and mild,
That is the little Jesus child.

Ah, Lord! the maker of us all,
How hast thou grown so poor and small?
There thou liest on withered grass—
The supper of the ox and ass.

Were the world wider many fold,
And decked with gems and cloth of gold,
'Twere far to mean and narrow all
To make for thee a cradle small.

Rough hay, and linen not too fine
Are the silk and velvet that are thine.
Yet as if they were thy kingdom great,
Thou liest in them in royal state.

And this, all this, hath pleasèd Thee,
That Thou mightst bring this truth to me:
That all earth's good, in one combined,
Is nothing to Thy mighty mind.

Ah, little Jesus, lay thy head
Down in a soft, white, little bed
That waits thee in this heart of mine,
And then this heart is always thine.

Such gladness in my heart would make
Me dance and sing for thy sweet sake.
Glory to God in highest heaven,
For he to us his Son hath given!

December 25

Thou hast not made, or taught me, Lord, to care
For times and seasons—but this one glad day
Is the blue sapphire clasping all the lights
That flash in the girdle of the year so fair—
When thou wast born a man, because alway
Thou wast and art a man, through all the flights
Of thought, and time, and thousandfold creation's play.

76882683R00091

Made in the USA
Columbia, SC
27 September 2019

A Christmas Carol

Babe Jesus lay in Mary's lap,
  The sun shone in his hair;
And this is how she saw, mayhap,
  The crown already there.

For she sang: "Sleep on, my little king;
  Bad Herod dares not come;
Before thee sleeping, holy thing,
  The wild winds would be dumb."

"I kiss thy hands, I kiss thy feet,
  My child, so long desired;
Thy hands will never be soiled, my sweet;
  Thy feet will never be tired."

"For thou art the king of men, my son;
  Thy crown I see it plain!
And men shall worship thee, every one,
  And cry, Glory! Amen"

Babe Jesus he opened his eyes wide—
  At Mary looked her lord.
Mother Mary stinted her song and sighed;
  Babe Jesus said never a word.

holy fool
press

$12 USA

ISBN 9781479284757

90000 >

9 781479 284757